—— See No Love ——

SEE NO LOVE

═ Monette Cummings ═

WALKER AND COMPANY

NEW YORK

First published in the United States of America
in 1983 by the Walker Publishing Company, Inc.

Published simultaneously in Canada by John Wiley & Sons Canada,
Limited, Rexdale, Ontario.

ISBN: 0-8027-0738-6

Library of Congress Catalog Card Number: 82-63201

Printed in the United States of America

10 9 8 7 6 5 4 3 2 1

=1=

"YOU ARE NOT to wear them again under any circumstances. I do not intend to tell you again."

Her ladyship had already said the same words many times, and her daughter was certain that she would often do so again.

"Do you understand me?"

"But, Mama, I cannot see—"

The girl's protest was swept aside as impatiently as one might brush off an annoying insect.

"Cannot see, indeed. What a piece of nonsense that is. I should never have allowed your father to put such an idea into your head. You know that you were never used to talk in such a fashion as this before he took you to that doctor. Doctor! He may call himself that and put the words in gold letters upon his door, but charlatan would be a better name for him, if anyone should ask my thoughts upon the subject—which, of course, neither you nor your father could be bothered to do."

They would hear them whether or not they asked, Emily thought, as her mother paused for an instant to get her breath, then plunged ahead once more.

"Telling your father that there was something wrong with your eyes and that you ought to wear spectacles! He could see at a glance—you will notice that *he* did not claim to be unable to see—that he could bilk such a soft-headed man as your father out of some of his money by spinning him such a tale. Cannot see! I vow that never in my life have I heard anything so foolish as that. I forbid you to speak such—such *fustian*! You know very well, both of you, that nothing will ever bring *me* to believe anything of the sort. After all, I am your mother, and *I* can see with no trouble, so there is no reason that you cannot do the same if you will only make the effort.''

Aware that the tirade, which she had heard in one form or another since the day her mother had first seen her in her spectacles, would go on until Lady Harmon tired of repeating herself, Emily gazed in dismay at her mother. Or at least she looked in the direction from which the scolding voice was coming and supposed that the large figure which she could perceive so dimly was that of her mother.

There had been a number of times in the past when she had thought that she was speaking to her ladyship, only to find on closer inspection of the recipient of her remarks that she had actually been speaking to a piece of furniture, one of the housemaids, or, upon one awful occasion, the new curate. That was an episode which Emily would have given much to forget, but Lady Harmon would not permit her to do so.

It had developed into a most embarrassing experience on all sides, for she had been making a confidence of the most delicate nature—not at all the sort of thing which a lady would mention in the presence of any gentleman, especially to one of the cloth. Much more straitlaced than many of his calling, he had quite naturally been scandalised at hearing such words from a young female, especially from one whom he had been including in his plans for the future.

''It might be,'' he declared in shocked tones, ''that a priest would be accustomed to hearing of such matters in the confessional, but I am not a Papist, and I cannot believe that a young lady such as yourself would say such things to me, Miss Harmon.''

Made aware by the sound of his voice of the error she had committed, Emily began to blush and stammer, trying to explain how so ghastly a mistake had come about.

"I thought . . . I thought that you were my mother."

This statement failed to mollify him, since it was so patently false.

"If you had said that you mistook me for your father," he said sternly, "I might possibly have understood, although I cannot credit that you would say such things to *him*. But that you could at any time mistake me for her ladyship—really, Miss Harmon, I beg you not to compound the matter by such falsehoods."

There was some justification for his indignation, since he was unaware of the nature of Emily's problem. Indeed, much as he might boast—in a self-deprecating manner that fooled no one except a few gullible spinsters—of his wish to become a "good shepherd" to the members of his church, he actually had little understanding of any of the problems that the members of his flock might have.

The greater part of his thoughts was given in a most unclerical manner to his own betterment, and he had decided that marriage to Lord Harmon's daughter might well result in his lordship's exerting some influence on his behalf. A spare young man of unprepossessing appearance, he had been led by the flutterings of those same impressionable spinsters to think of himself as a handsome man, and he could see no reason why Miss Harmon should not be happy to accept his offer. He had come to the Hall that day with the express purpose of declaring himself, only to be met with such remarks from the girl he had intended to make his own as to overset him completely.

Emily was endeavouring to explain her inability to see when Lady Harmon came into the room, having been told that the gentleman had arrived and that her daughter was alone with him. This was decidedly improper, even if he was a man of the cloth. She greeted the curate pleasantly enough on that account, although she personally had little use for him, and offered him tea. However, he brushed past her, almost rudely, saying that he would return at some later date when he had been able to compose himself—silently vowing, as he did so, that no consideration could now induce him to offer for a female with a mind so wanton as Miss Harmon's.

When Lady Harmon enquired if something was troubling him, he snapped, "Your ladyship had best ask Miss Harmon about that. It is not a matter of which *I* should care to speak."

The moment the door closed behind him, Lady Harmon turned upon her daughter, wrathfully demanding the truth, and when Emily, who had long since given way to tears, confessed what had occurred, her mother scolded her thoroughly for her lack of sensibility, refusing to accept Emily's explanation as to the reason for its happening. The fact that she personally considered the curate to be a toadeater did not make her daughter's behaviour any the less appalling.

That had been only one *faux pas* among the many that Emily Harmon had committed during the years, so how could her mama—especially now—say that she had never mentioned the trouble with her vision, even though the girl had not realised at the time that she had more trouble than anyone else?

Such things as these never occurred when she wore the spectacles that Papa had recently bought her. She wished that she might do so always, but her mama, although reluctantly agreeing that she might wear them in the privacy of her room, had insisted from the first that Emily was *never* to have them on where she might be seen.

Her ladyship, at the first sight of her daughter in spectacles, had demanded her vinaigrette and, as soon as she had recovered somewhat from the shock, had declared, "You may be certain that no gentleman is going to offer for you if he sees you with those disgusting things upon your face."

It is most unlikely that anyone will offer for me anyway, Emily said, but only to herself, for if her mama had heard the words, there would certainly have been another scold for her lack of sensibility, one of Emily's most common faults in Lady Harmon's eyes. The girl, however, could see nothing wrong in rating her attractions so low, unless it would be someone like old General Mayling, who was forever trying to pinch her. It would never be anyone that she might care for. She had convinced herself—*almost* convinced herself—that this did not matter. The fact that she had escaped a proposal from the curate was unknown and, had she known, she would only have been thankful that it was so.

How could *anyone* ever learn to care for me? she had asked herself time after time, trying to examine her reflexion in the mirror. Since her face would be pressed tightly against the glass, all that she could observe was a flattened nose and a pair of large, peculiarly shaped eyes. They were an odd colour, as well. She was unaware of the creaminess of her complexion and of the tiny, even teeth that were revealed whenever she smiled, nor did she know what a pretty shape her nose had when it was not flattened against the mirror.

From the time that Emily had been a small child, almost everyone who saw her—excepting only those mamas who were jealous enough to prefer their own daughters' appearance—had remarked upon the size and brilliance of her eyes. As she grew older, several very young gentlemen were heard to praise the length of her lashes as well. No one, least of all the child, realised that there was anything about her eyes which was out of the common way.

Since no one had mentioned the fact to her, how was she to know that everyone did not see the same blurred images that she saw? To her, people did not have faces—in fact, they scarcely had forms—until she was quite close to them.

Trees, fences, and even buildings sprang suddenly out of nowhere as she moved about, then disappeared just as quickly. It had always happened that way; she expected such things even if she did not understand the reason for them.

Through the years, she had become quite accustomed to falling over unseen objects in her path—objects that others seemed to be able to avoid quite easily—but merely thought that she was as clumsy as her mama and her governesses declared her to be. When Miss Tompkins, who was the worst of all the dragons inflicted upon her, frequently rapped her upon the head and ordered, "Sit up, Emily—you must remember that you are a young lady, not a charity child— and study your lessons," Emily would straighten obediently, then lean down again as soon as she might.

"She does not like me and is only looking for some reason to scold me," the girl would mutter beneath her breath. "*Anyone* knows it is quite impossible to do both at once."

Several teachers had despaired of teaching her to play the spinet, but after they had—figuratively, except in the case of Miss Tompkins—thrown up their hands, she had learnt to play the instrument well enough to entertain herself at times by bending down to see the music and picking out one note at a time until she had memorised several of the simpler pieces and could recognise the notes by touch.

She felt quite proud of this accomplishment, but could not be persuaded to play before others. When some other young lady entertained with a lengthy sonata that was beyond her ability, Emily blamed her own failure upon her faulty memory and silently accepted her mama's scolds for refusing to take part in these musical evenings.

She was vaguely aware that certain gentlemen—she could recognise them if they were near enough because their shapes were different from those of the ladies in their gowns— walked in the direction of the spinet when the ladies played. However, she assumed that it was only out of a desire for their company, since she could not see that these attentive gentlemen were turning the pages of the music as an excuse for their presence.

* * *

It was on the eve of her sixteenth birthday, when her mama was making elaborate plans for her come-out, that Lord Harmon brought home a visitor for dinner, unaware that he was bringing a change into his daughter's life. Ordered to join her parents and the guest in the drawing room, Emily entered the room confidently. At the expense of a number of painful bruises, she had memorised the location of each piece of furniture scattered about the room, and she started across the room in the direction of the voices. She had no way of knowing that a footstool had been removed from its usual position and was now directly in her path.

The visitor, an eminent doctor, was the only one to notice the danger. Stepping to the girl's side, he caught her arm and guided her away from the object. Emily was inclined to resent what appeared to be undue familiarity until the gentleman explained in a low voice what had happened.

After dinner, the ladies retired, and Emily received a scold from her ladyship for trying to attract the visitor's attention in such a manner—a scold of which the girl did not hear a single word, for she was trying to solve the puzzle of how the visitor could have known of the presence of the footstool when she did not.

Left alone with Lord Harmon, the doctor barely took a sip of his lordship's excellent port before saying, "My lord, when you showed me about your acres today, I was greatly impressed, observing the care which you lavish upon your estates and how you have the welfare of your tenants at heart. Having seen this, I am astonished when I find that you have made no effort to alleviate your daughter's myopia."

The word was one his lordship had never heard, but, in common with all medical terms, it had an ominous sound. In his own, somewhat careless way, he was quite fond of his daughter and he bristled at what he considered to be censure in the other's tone and said, "I can assure you, sir, that never would I be guilty of neglecting anything which would add to my daughter's well-being. You abuse your position as a guest in my house when you imply that I would do such a thing."

"I apologise, Lord Harmon, if it sounded to you as though I was accusing you of neglect. However, I must confess that, in a way, that is exactly what I was doing. I pray you will forgive me."

Lord Harmon grunted an acceptance of this odd apology and refilled both glasses.

"What I intended by my first remark was that it surprised me that neither you nor her ladyship appear to be aware of a condition which obviously has existed for some time. Perhaps you have been too near to it, and it takes a stranger—a medical man—to see it. The truth is, my lord, that your daughter *cannot* see—or at least, she can see things only when they are very close to her eyes."

He drained his glass, but shook his head to an offer of more wine as he continued, "I can see that you find this difficult to believe, but certainly you must have been aware this evening that she was unable to tell there was a footstool in her path and would have fallen over it if I had not forestalled her. I should be willing to wager that if we were to go into the next room and stand before her, saying nothing, she would not be able to tell which of us is which."

"If I did not know that you have had only a glass and a half of port, I should say that you were foxed," declared his host. "Not tell us apart? Man, we look nothing at all alike, and certainly Emily could tell her own papa."

"Anyone else could certainly do so, I admit. But Miss Harmon would not be able to tell. Your daughter, my lord, should be wearing spectacles."

Lord Harmon was inclined to ridicule this remark as well. A dowager might employ a *face-à-main*, but the thought of a young lady in spectacles was not to be considered.

He was, however, a reasonable man and the doctor's words remained in his mind. For the next several days, he studied

Emily's actions closely, a thing he had not troubled himself to do before, since he considered that it was his wife's place to oversee their daughter's upbringing. He could see the truth and, despite Lady Harmon's protests—which were loud indeed—he took Emily to the man and had her fitted for spectacles.

To Emily, it was as if someone had opened up an entirely different world to her. For the first time, she realised that trees had leaves and flowers had petals—had them all of the time and not only when they were immediately before her eyes—instead of being merely the blobs of colour they had previously appeared.

She also discovered that she could tell one person from another, even on the far side of the room, and that strange objects no longer made their unsuspected way into her path. Despite the discomfort of having an object perched upon her nose, which during the first weeks felt that it must weigh a stone or more, she welcomed her spectacles for all of the new wonders they brought her.

Compared to her own ambitions for Emily, none of these matters was of the slightest importance to Lady Harmon. Her ladyship was no more, and no less, inconsiderate than any other mother whose aim in life was to see her daughter successfully married—"successfully" meaning to someone of higher rank, if possible. Emily had beauty, even though she herself did not believe it; she had an amiable disposition, despite her mama's frequent accusations to the contrary; she had an ancient if not illustrious lineage. But finding an acceptable suitor for her would not be easy. The competition was too great, and the young ladies with the largest dowries would be the first to have handkerchiefs thrown their way.

By any standards, Emily's dowry could be called no more than comfortable—especially with the expense of keeping her brother at university—so it was important that she make the best of every asset she did possess. And in Lady Harmon's mind, her daughter's spectacles would be no asset. Far otherwise.

"How do you think we shall ever be able to find a husband—any husband—for Emily if she is permitted to go about looking as she does now?" she railed at her husband. "Why, she looks positively deformed with those thick spectacles upon her nose. You may as well resign yourself to having her remain a spinster."

His lordship would have had no objection to such a state of affairs, for he had always found his daughter most companionable. His son was something of a disappointment to a bookish man, but had, with a great deal of forceful tutoring, finally been accepted at Oxford.

What good that would do, Lord Harmon could not see, but his lady had been eager for their son to attend so illustrious an institution. George had gone with reluctance; he did not like books, and it was doubtful that he had opened one since leaving home, so his father considered that his chance of earning any honours was nonexistent. On the other hand, Emily had read a great deal in the years when there were so few other things she could do, and was able to enter into discussions with her father upon politics, business, and many other subjects far beyond the ken of the average young female.

This erudition upon her daughter's part was another thing that frightened Lady Harmon. What if Emily should launch into some of those topics before others and word began to get around that she was *blue*? Fatal!

Much as he would have liked to keep her with him, Lord Harmon could understand that it would be unfair to Emily if she were not permitted, even encouraged, to find a husband. It was not to be thought of that she should dwindle into a spinster aunt to George's future children.

Also, he had a great dislike of family squabbles. Her ladyship might reiterate—frequently—that she had said everything about the matter that she intended to say, but her husband knew better. Amelia had never yet abandoned a subject until she had got her own way. Weakly, he agreed to her dictum that Emily was never to wear her spectacles in public.

"But they do me no good if I cannot wear them," the girl had protested only once. She had received such a scold that she never repeated the offense.

At first, she obeyed the command not to appear outside her room with the spectacles, but after her papa had agreed that she might wear them when they were alone together in the library—the one place they were safe from Mama's intrusion, but also the one place where Emily felt that she needed them the least—she began to escape out of doors with them from time to time.

There were so many wonderful things to be seen out here that she had never known to exist. A series of scrabbling sounds, which had sometimes frightened her in the past, was discovered to be nothing more ominous than a pair of squirrels frolicking about a tree trunk. She watched them until their antics made her laugh, which frightened them into hiding.

It was delightful to roam among the flowers and be able to tell one from another, to watch the birds flitting from branch to branch among the trees, to see a flock of sheep grazing upon a far hill. Even with her spectacles, these last were none too clear, but at least she knew they were there, and she had not known before.

No amount of chastisement by her mama prevented these excursions, and at last Lady Harmon was brought to agree that Emily might wear the spectacles as often as she liked when they still remained at Harmon Hall, since she had seen that the girl was careful to whisk them out of sight when visitors approached. The servants already knew of them, of course, as they knew everything that went on in the house, but none of them would wish to spoil the young lady's chances of a good match, so they forbore to pass on such an interesting piece of gossip to the neighbour's servants.

Since she had failed in her attempts to make Emily keep her spectacles in her room—or better still, not to wear them at all—Lady Harmon cleverly made use of the fact.

"If I permit you to have them now," she said, "you must promise me that they will never appear on your nose while we are in London."

"I promise, I promise," Emily said recklessly, happy to have won such a concession from her ladyship. As a result, she went through the next several months gazing intently but unseeingly at a blur of unknown people.

Lady Harmon had by now been reluctantly forced to admit—to herself—that her daughter had difficulty in seeing, but she stubbornly clung to the belief that if she did not admit that the disability existed, it might magically disappear. Still, she kept a careful eye upon the girl and only once was unable to prevent her from curtsying to an overcorpulent manservant in the mistaken belief that he was the Prince Regent.

There was another occasion, of course, when she was discovered flirting her fan and addressing a series of complimentary remarks to a basket of flowers adorning a pillar, wondering as she did so why her companion said nothing. No one else had noticed her, however, and her ladyship was able to guide her quickly away, so no harm was done.

Lady Harmon was never told of one near-catastrophe, and Emily herself was not aware of the narrowness of her escape. On the day when she was to have the final fitting for her presentation gown, her mama—after delaying the dread deed for as long as possible—was forced to go to the dentist to have a tooth drawn. Emily set out, therefore, in the company of a young housemaid and the family coachman, who was instructed to return for them in an hour.

The fitting was completed in less than half that time, and

the servant, whose name was Molly and who was keeping company with a footman from the house next door, said hesitantly, "If you wouldn't mind, miss—seeing that we have to wait—could I run around the corner to a little shop I know of? Tomorrow's me free afternoon, and I'd like a new riband for me bonnet. The old one's gone all to bits."

"Certainly," Emily told her, knowing how strict the housekeeper was about allowing the girls to have any additional free time. "But I must go with you. I cannot wait here alone."

"Oh, I know, miss. That wouldn't never do," Molly gasped. Aware that her mistress would not be able to see how poor the shop would be, she saw no harm in taking her there. Grasping Emily's hand, she guided her along to the place, which was indeed far down the scale from Madame Elva's select establishment, despite its nearness to the better shops.

There was a large crowd in the shop, and as Molly haggled over the cost of the bit of riband she wanted, Emily was pushed away from the maid. Knowing that Molly would find her in a short time, she stood waiting till a voice at her side said sympathetically, "Lost, are ye, dearie?"

"No, no," Emily said quickly, startled that a stranger should accost her in this manner, but fortunately unable to see the raddled cheeks, orange hair, and tawdry finery of the other. "I am waiting . . . for someone."

"And likely he ain't comin'." The sympathy was stronger now. "Though why anyone would desert a pretty thing like ye, it's hard to see. Most probably, he got into a game with some of his friends and lost all his blunt. But no need to worry yer pretty head. Just come along with Auntie and she'll take ye to a nice place where there'll be gents willin' to give ye all sorts of pretties."

She put her hand upon Emily's arm, thinking this was a lucky day for her after all. There had not been a single green country girl on any of the coaches she had met, and she had despaired of finding the fresh merchandise many of her customers insisted upon having. And then to come upon such a pretty girl standing about here, just waiting to be taken, as if it had been planned. . . .

Emily tried to pull free from the grasp that tightened upon her arm, crying, "No, I shall not. Molly!"

Her voice had risen to a shriek, and the servant dropped her bit of riband and pushed her way quickly to her mistress's side. No stranger to London, she was immediately aware of the sort of person who had hold of Miss Emily, and flew at the woman, hitting her with her bag and crying, "Leave her be, ye old hag! Can ye not reckernize Quality when ye see it?"

Realising from the arrival of the maidservant that she had indeed made a mistake, the woman released Emily's arm and hurried away, fearing that a call would be made to take her up. If the girl *was* Quality—and she did not doubt it now— taking her would be called abduction and would earn her transportation, if not the noose. No girl was worth such a risk; her customers would have to make do with the girls she had.

Any thought of completing her own purchase forgotten in her fright, Molly caught Emily by the hand and hurried her back to Madame Elva's, arriving before the shop just as Thomas tooled the carriage around the corner. As he drew to a stop and Molly held the door for her mistress, she said in a low tone, "If ye don't mind, miss, it might be best if ye didn't say nothing about our going to that shop." In her terror, the girl had reverted to the speech of her childhood. "If her ladyship was to find out that I'd left ye even for a minute, I'd be turned off for sure."

And if she hadn't been quick enough getting back to Miss Emily's side and that old—*thing*— had succeeded in dragging the girl off to some brothel, Molly knew she would have killed herself—if his lordship hadn't killed her first.

Still overset by the old woman's attempt to carry her off, but totally unaware of her purpose, Emily nodded agreement. Lady Harmon would doubtless turn the girl off without a character, just as she feared. Also, she would be angry with her daughter for allowing herself to be taken to a shop which, even without being able to see it, Emily knew was not the sort of place to which she should have gone.

So the two arrived home, Molly to flee below stairs and Emily to report to her mama that Elva had promised the gown would be finished in time. Lying down with a cold cloth on her aching jaw, Lady Harmon only told her to hurry and dress because Lady Sefton had kindly offered to stop and take her to Almack's this evening—but first to call Hough and tell her to fetch her mistress some laudanum.

Emily sometimes wondered why she should attend Almack's or go to balls. Much as she enjoyed listening to the music, there was little else she could do at such places. She did not dance. Her mama disapproved of the waltz, and Emily's one attempt at the quadrille had been disastrous, as she had not been able to locate her partner or to see where she was to go.

Still, sitting upon the sidelines did not appear to interfere with her popularity. There were any number of young gentlemen who were willing to sit beside such a pretty girl and bask in what they believed to be her adoring glances, or to bring her as many glasses of lemonade as she could be induced to accept. None of them noticed that Emily was careful never to call them by name, as she could not tell one of them from another.

2

TO THE SURPRISE of everyone, especially herself, the Honourable Miss Emily Harmon managed to get through her presentation successfully, although Lady Harmon quaked in fear the entire time, aware that Emily might trip and fling herself into the sovereign's lap.

The sooner I can find her a husband, she told herself, the better it will be. Once she is safely married, any of her errors will be her husband's responsibility, not mine.

In her own youth, Lady Harmon had been a pale, pretty girl, even in those days inclined toward plumpness and with an extreme fondness for sweets and pastries. These her mother had kept away from her as much as possible during her several seasons. The girl and her mother had almost despaired of finding her a husband when she had caught the eye of the eldest son of a baron, who was thankfully accepted.

Mr. Harmon had, in time, inherited his father's estates and title, and his lady, having presented him with an heir—who was now frittering away his time and his father's money at Oxford—and a daughter, had felt free to indulge her appetites to the fullest. The result was an increase in her girth which made it difficult for her to get about.

Her husband, on the other hand, had been a spare man when they were married and had grown more so as the years went by. At one time, he had remarked in a jocular mood that if the pair of them were not careful, people would begin to think that she had been taking his food. Her ladyship, however, had no sense of humour and, as she had been able to convince herself that she was not *very* fat, she had been deeply hurt by the comment. Unwilling to wound her sensibilities, Lord Harmon had never repeated the remark, but he thought of it from time to time and smiled at it privately.

Lady Harmon had also convinced herself that her daughter's wish to wear her spectacles was much the same sort of thing as her own craving for rich foods, something which must be hidden until she was safely married. In fact, she had often thought that a dowry of reasonable size might cause any number of gentlemen to overlook plumpness in choosing a wife, while it would certainly take a fortune, which Emily did not possess, to overcome the effect of those disfiguring spectacles. As Lady Jersey herself had said, upon glimpsing an impoverished gentlewoman who was serving as companion to a mutual friend, "That poor creature—what can she expect of life if she must hide behind those spectacles? Who would have her? Some country parson, perhaps, or a recluse with his head in his books so that he need not see his pitiful wife."

That, from one of the leaders of the ton. Certainly no one must be allowed to say such a thing of Emily.

Unknown to Lady Harmon, the reason that Emily had come through her presentation with no mishaps was due in great part to the fact that she had stood near a Lady Violet Leslie, who appeared to understand something of Emily's problem. When they began to take their places, she whispered commands, telling Emily where she was to go, when she should curtsy, and what pitfalls should be avoided.

The ceremony of presentation was an ordeal to every young girl, but was so much worse for Emily that she was near to collapse by the time they had escaped the Presence. Lady Violet caught her arm and guided her to a seat, saying sympathetically, "Would you have believed it if anyone had told you how ghastly such an affair could be? I cannot understand how any of us managed to live through it."

"At least you were able to see what you were doing," Emily said bitterly, thinking for the first time that her mama was being unfair in pitchforking her into such a trial as she had just been forced to endure without even allowing her the compensation of being able to see what had occurred. "Was it the queen to whom we were presented, or one of the princesses?"

"The queen, of course. . . . Oh, you mean that you did not *know*?" Lady Violet asked, seating herself at Emily's side. "Is it truly as bad as that?"

Emily nodded and leaned forward so that she could see something of her new acquaintance. If only she had her spectacles so that she could tell. . . . Still, now that she understood, the other young lady did not seem to mind being stared at in such a fashion.

Lady Violet was well accustomed to being stared at, although not at such close range. She had reason to be somewhat vain of her appearance, having a profusion of black ringlets falling about a face that one admirer had described as heart-shaped. She had been told by another that her brown eyes danced; at the moment, they did not do so, being full of sympathy for her companion.

Looking carefully at Lady Violet, Emily sighed. This was the sort of colouring she had always wished for herself. Her own was insipid, she thought, being unable to see the golden lights that sunshine frequently struck from her hair, the nearly perfect oval of her face, the slight tilt of her nose when it was not pressed against the mirror, or the soft curve of her lips. She had not looked at herself while she was wearing her spectacles, fearful that she would appear as ugly in them as her mama said. To her, her hair was merely light brown and her eyes a disappointing shade of dark blue.

"Oh, they are not blue at all; they are almost purple. Pansy-coloured," her ladyship exclaimed when Emily confided her unhappiness with her features. "And I love the shape of your nose. If mine only looked like that. But by the time I am thirty, I shall certainly have the Leslie beak—just

23

like Aunt Helen. I suppose it does not matter in one so old, but May has it, too, so I am certain to go the same way."

The truth was that Lady Helen Leslie had inherited "the beak" from her maternal ancestors, not from the Leslies, and had passed it to her daughter. Lady Violet's nose was tiny and attractive, without the slightest tendency toward beakiness, but, girl-like, she wished that it had a different shape.

"Let us be friends," she said impulsively. "Do say that you will."

"Certainly, I should like that." Emily was aware, even as she spoke that, once separated from the other girl, she would not be able to recognise her if they should meet a second time, and might easily cut her at some future function.

"My parents have promised that we are to have a house party as soon as the season is over. You must come; I shall insist upon it. I am certain that my brother will be wild—" She coloured at having allowed a cant term to slip into her speech, but Emily did not see. "I mean, most happy to meet you. You will like him, too, I am certain. He is very nice, even if he *is* my brother."

Lady Violet really did not think her brother such a paragon, considering instead that he was something of a dolt, given to all sorts of foolishness, such as the foppish attire he had recently begun wearing. He also thought his five years' seniority gave him the right to order her about. However, on the strength of two hours' acquaintance, she had decided that Emily would make a perfect sister-in-law. Surely, if *they* were good friends, Emily could overlook dullness in a husband—that was, if Arthur would have the sense to see how perfect she was for him.

"I am certain that he must be if he is *your* brother," Emily said, for, like Lady Violet, she had felt an immediate kinship, which occurs so rarely between a pair of young ladies. She did not think, however, that the other girl's talk of an invitation was anything more than an attempt to put her at ease; she doubted that Lady Violet would be permitted to issue invitations to any chance acquaintance. She did not mention it at home, merely telling her mama that she had met Lady Violet Leslie, who had been very kind to her.

Lady Violet, who was very much a creature of impulse, had immediately begged her parents to include Emily Harmon and *her* parents in the house party. She did not confide her plans for her brother and her new friend, thinking it might prejudice the countess against the girl. As soon as her mama had a chance to meet Emily, Lady Violet was certain she would agree that here was the perfect wife for Arthur.

The earl was anxious to return to the country as quickly as possible. It was the first time in years that he had been away from his prize-winning roses for so long a time. Nothing less than his daughter's presentation could have taken him away, and he was convinced that, in his absence, the gardener would not be giving the plants proper care.

"Do as you like, Miranda," he said. "I leave the matter in your capable hands."

"Naturally," the countess replied, having intended to please herself, for the earl could never be depended upon to interest himself in such matters. He would appear at the party from time to time, then would disappear into the garden to search his roses for signs of mildew or some other blight.

Eager to indulge her daughter whenever possible, the countess set discreet enquiries afoot. Learning that Baron and Lady Harmon were quite above reproach, she decided that their daughter might be an excellent companion for Violet, and the invitation was issued.

Emily's surprise was no greater than Lady Harmon's delight at the receipt of the crested missive inviting the family—with the exception of George, who was still, it was hoped, at Oxford and not into some expensive mischief—to a house party at Maidencourt.

"What an excellent opportunity this will be for Emily, especially as she did not receive an offer during the season —at least not an eligible one," her ladyship exclaimed, thinking of the two offers that Lord Harmon had refused to consider. Neither of the suitors was truly ineligible, but Harmon had been right to refuse them; a baron's daughter, with better—if far distant—connexions on her mama's side, should be able to do better than that.

"I do not understand why you do not make more of an effort to attract their attention, girl," she complained. "Anyone would think you *wished* to remain on the shelf."

"Hardly on the shelf when she ain't even seventeen," his lordship said mildly, but the comment was ignored.

"There are certain to be any number of young gentlemen present at such a party. We must see Elva and have some new gowns made for you at once."

While he was far from being miserly, Lord Harmon grunted at the thought of this additional expense, and his daughter said, "But, Mama, I have at least a half dozen gowns that I have never worn."

She knew that they were beautiful gowns, for when she was alone she had donned her spectacles (surely, her promise to her mama not to wear them in the city did not count when no one could see her) and had examined each one of them. Although all her gowns were white, as befit a young lady in her first season, no two were alike. They were skillfully embroidered and trimmed. Several had coloured sashes or ruffling. Emily was unable to tell how much they became her, but she thought they should do very well for the house party.

Her mama brushed the comment aside as unimportant, her mind having proceeded to another matter.

"I wonder if the viscount will be present," she mused. "It would be too much to hope for the duke, even if he should decide to honour the party with his presence. I have heard from Lady Jersey, who knows everything that goes on in the ton—and tells what she knows to anyone who will listen, and to many who will not—that he is expected to offer for Lady Isobel Darcy almost any day. But the viscount. . . ."

Having inherited her father's sense of humour, Emily was tempted to ask which viscount her mama had in mind, for

26

there must have been at least a dozen of various ages and stages of availability among the notables she had met during the season. Lady Harmon would not have appreciated the jest, however, so Emily merely smiled at the thought and said, "I think that he may be expected to be there. Lady Violet did make some mention that she would like for me to meet her brother."

She did not add Lady Violet's comment that her brother would be "wild" to meet Emily. This she considered only the young lady's enthusiasm for a new friend and thought it more than likely that, in the crowd of the house party, she and Lord Stearnes might not even be introduced. The little she did say was more than enough to send her mama into alt.

"Why did you not tell me that at once, you foolish child? Can you not see what it must mean? Her ladyship must know the sort of young lady her brother prefers, and if she wishes you to meet him, it can mean only one thing. Emily, you must do everything within your power to fix his interest during the party. It is unlikely that you will ever have another opportunity half as good as this."

"Mama, I do not even know the gentleman. It might be that I would take him in dislike—"

"Take him in dislike? What a piece of nonsense! How could it be possible for you to do such a thing? He is a most eligible gentleman, and I am told he is quite handsome as well."

At least she *thought* the informant who had said so had been speaking of Arthur Leslie, the young Lord Stearnes; but even if she had not, what did it matter? Appearances counted for much less than blue blood in the marriage market, and the viscount could boast of that if he chose.

"You have told me how much you like Lady Violet, so it stands to reason that you will like her brother when you meet him. Remember, too, that he is heir to an earldom and—until Durban sets up his nursery—to a dukedom as well. What a coup it would be if you could bring him to make you an offer during the party. You may be certain that Lady Violet will see that there are opportunities in plenty for you to be together. But you must do your part. Look your prettiest; and on no account are you to wear those dreadful spectacles. I absolutely forbid it. Do you understand me?"

"I am certain, my dear," Lord Harmon said mildly, relieving his daughter of the necessity of answering this familiar speech, "that everyone in the house has understood you. I fear you sometimes forget how . . . how the sound carries in this old building," he finished lamely, aware of the angry glint in his wife's eyes.

Nonetheless, Lady Harmon had received his message. There might be servants in the London house who were less devoted to the idea of getting Emily married than those at the Hall, and if they should spread the word that Emily wore spectacles, the fault would not be Emily's, but her own.

She said nothing more for the moment, but repeated her warning many times as the days went by, careful, however, not to allow the servants to overhear her. Madame Elva had fallen victim to a bout of influenza, so Lady Harmon decided that, with the proper patterns, local seamstresses could fit Emily's new gowns with no trouble. To Lord Harmon's relief, they could also do it much more cheaply than the London dressmakers. He begrudged nothing that would make his daughter a success, but there were times when he wondered if it was necessary for her to have *quite* so many new gowns. After all, there were George's bills to be paid, too.

As for Emily, with the date of the house party drawing nearer day by day, she found that she was looking forward to the occasion with as much apprehension as pleasure. She was happy at the thought of continuing her acquaintance with Lady Violet, but she wished heartily that she had never mentioned her ladyship's desire that Emily meet her brother.

From the moment she had heard those words, Lady Harmon's conversation—in private, of course—had dwelt almost entirely upon the desirability of her daughter's bringing young Viscount Stearnes up to scratch. Her ladyship would not have used those words, for she abhorred sporting cant. But Emily, who had learnt the term from her brother, George, thought that her mama's meaning was the same.

The moment that the family returned to London, word of the impending visit had spread below stairs, and the servants' hall was buzzing with discussions of Miss Emily's chances. Nothing of any import was known about the viscount, which was surprising, as the servants usually knew everything. What they did know was that he was heir to the Earl of Montayne and cousin to the "Dook" of Durban. Such a relationship was not to be sneezed at and all of them were certain their young lady could pull it off if she put her mind to it.

The only one in doubt of her ability to do so was the young lady herself. She had not succeeded too well in attracting eligible young men to the point of offering for her. By no means was every young lady promised by the end of her first season; even some of the Incomparables failed in this respect. Still, Lady Harmon had considered it laxness on her daughter's part that she had not done so.

The invitation to the house party changed all that. Her ladyship had wondered privately if Lord Harmon had not been just the slightest bit hasty in dismissing the earlier offers so firmly. Perhaps he ought to have held out some hope that he would change his mind. Now she saw how wise he had been.

"Nothing particularly clever about not wishing to have either of those young nodcocks in the family," his lordship protested, but this comment was waved away by his wife, who said, "It *was* clever, believe me, for now Emily can do so much better for herself if only she will make the proper effort."

Emily sighed, but made no reply to this. It would have been useless, for Mama had made up her mind that her daughter was to be a viscountess.

There must be an art to casting out lures to gentlemen, Emily supposed, for she had been unable to see how any of the other young ladies went about this occupation. For that matter, she was not even certain that she wished to attract Lord Stearnes. Of course, if he should be as charming as his sister, she knew she would like him; but liking someone and wishing to marry him were two different matters. Her mama could condemn her for a romantic little fool, but Emily dreamed, in a hazy sort of way, of meeting a man she could love.

"Love," Lady Harmon would have declared, "is for shop-girls and servants. You will become fond enough of your husband, and that is all that matters." So Emily said nothing of her dreams.

In a volume devoted to stately homes, she had found a picture of Maidencourt and was frightened by the thought of trying to find her way about so large a house without her spectacles—which, of course, her mama would not allow her to wear. There would be great numbers of strangers to meet, and she could never be certain whether the strangers were laughing at something she could not see, or at her blunders.

Unaware that Lady Harmon had dispatched an acceptance on the day the invitation had arrived, she thought of going to her papa and begging him to refuse the invitation. He would do so if he thought the visit would make his daughter unhappy, but the pair of them would be in for endless scoldings about Emily's lost chances, and his lordship would be finding himself blamed for having ruined his daughter's life.

"I cannot do that to him," the girl said with a sigh. "Poor Papa—his peace would be cut up entirely. It always is when Mama is in one of her moods. And I *should* like to see Violet again. Perhaps I am making too much of the matter."

= 3 =

THE SEAMSTRESSES WERE already hard at work on Emily's new gowns for the party. Now that her first season was behind her, her mama had decided that she might wear some of the colours that became her so well. Not bright colours, of course—those would still be frowned upon for one so young—but soft pinks, blues, and yellows, cut and draped to give only a hint of the figure beneath them. She must appeal to the viscount, but not blatantly.

There would be no extreme décolletage for her daughter, Lady Harmon ordered, and no "invisible petticoats." The local seamstresses agreed, shocked by the mention of such scandalous garments. Emily, to whom petticoats and all other items of clothing were almost invisible anyway, was completely unaware of the extremely immodest garments displayed by—and displaying—some of the more daring ladies of the ton, could not understand the reason for their shock.

Lord Harmon had been persuaded to purchase a new and stylish town carriage at the beginning of the season, and his lady found herself unable to convince him that a new travelling carriage was a necessity for the visit.

"Styles in carriages do not change so much," he said, a statement with which she argued uselessly. "A little brushing up is all this one needs. Unless you would prefer a new carriage to more gowns for Emily."

As he had expected, this last argument—which he would never have put into effect—was enough to silence his wife, and the old carriage was brought out. The "brushing up" soon extended to include a bright new coat of paint and additional gilt upon the crest, and since the squabs showed little sign of wear, even her ladyship could scarcely complain that the carriage was shabby. It was well sprung also, for it had been built to his lordship's own direction, and he preferred to travel—when it was necessary for him to do so—in comfort.

Emily had not been the only member of the family to search out the picture of Maidencourt. Her mama had looked at it with much more satisfaction than the girl had felt and had read the accompanying text, although it was not her habit to read anything other than *La Belle Assemblée* and the court calendar.

However, she felt that her perusal of the article was worth her trouble when she learnt that Maidencourt had been the residence of the Dukes of Durban and had been given to his brother by the fifth duke. Nothing was said about the service to the crown that had enabled Edmund Leslie to rise—before he had retired to devote his time to his roses—from a mere "lordship" as the second son of the fourth duke to the earldom of Montayne. Lady Harmon was not disappointed that no details of the rise were given; the end result was interesting enough in itself.

The description given in the book of the mansion and grounds was impressive, but as the carriage passed between the massive stone gateposts with their heraldic animals, her ladyship became aware that what she had read fell far short of reality. Maidencourt was an estate of many hundreds of acres and, as the Harmons were driven along the gravelled drive toward the house, Lady Harmon gazed upon the expanse of parkland and shrubbery with satisfaction, imagining the day when her daughter would be mistress of all this.

She would have denied indignantly any charge that she was ambitious and told herself that it was not for her own aggrandizement that she coveted this estate. After all, as a mother, it was natural for her to wish only the best for her child. And to her mind, the best to which Emily could aspire was to become in time the Countess of Montayne and owner of all this property.

The fact that she would then be mother-in-law to the earl was not important—or at least she told herself that it was not.

"Look at that, Emily," she commanded, pointing shamelessly, since there was no one about who might see this vulgar action on her part. "There are swans upon the lake. Are they not beautiful? I vow we shall have to have some at the Hall. I am certain, too, that white spot among the trees is a folly built in the shape of a Grecian temple. One can only wonder how far this estate must extend."

Since the pointing hand had come directly before her face, Emily obediently turned her head in the direction indicated. She supposed the lake must be where the green blur that was the grass gave way to a lighter colour. The swans she would have been unable to recognise even if they had been beside the carriage, and she could not discern the faintest glimmer to show where the folly might lie.

She knew that it would be useless for her to say so, however; her mama would merely repeat that if *she* could see these things, there was no reason why Emily could not do so as well. It had taken some time for Lady Harmon to admit, even to herself, that her daughter's eyesight was far from perfect. Nonetheless, she still behaved as if, by saying nothing of the affliction, she could cause it to disappear. The only thing necessary was for Emily to make an effort to see.

Unaware of this convoluted reasoning on her mama's part, Emily said to herself, She seems to think that I purposely do not see them.

Seated opposite the pair, Lord Harmon had observed his wife's gesture and Emily's expression, and he shook his head. No more than her ladyship was he able to understand why Emily had trouble in seeing; unlike her, he accepted the fact. He was not surprised by Amelia's attitude. Twenty years of life with her had taught him that when she set her mind upon something, there was nothing which could change it—least of all, logic.

Perhaps he ought to have put his foot down—something he did as seldom as possible—and insisted that Emily should be allowed to wear her spectacles on this visit. Still, what if Amelia *was* right—for once—and they would interfere with the child's getting a husband? It would be better for her to be unhappy for a time than to have her entire life ruined. He sighed, causing his wife to shoot a suspicious look in his direction, but by that time he was looking fixedly at something outside the carriage window, so she supposed that he must only be as envious of Maidencourt's grandeur as she was.

Even Emily could scarcely fail to be aware of the great size of the building they were now approaching. Of weathered grey stone—the older parts showing more signs of weathering than the later additions—it reached upward out of her sight and stretched for what appeared to be a great distance on either side of the huge front door. Remembering the pictures, she determined that she would creep out sometime when no one was about, put on her spectacles—for she had slipped them into her reticule despite her mama's orders to leave them at home—and take a good look at it. She had never seen a mansion, for the Hall was not large enough to be called by that name, and she had no opportunity to see the buildings in London.

A footman in the dark blue and gold Montayne livery held the carriage door and helped the visitors to alight. Having spent a great deal of time before the journey in practising how to get in and out of the carriage without falling, Emily knew exactly how far she must step down, and she reached the ground without mishap. However, she would have tripped upon the first of the three shallow steps leading up to the doorway if Lady Violet had not come running out to fling her arms about her friend.

Emily, having been able to recognise her during the embrace, made the introductions, and Lady Violet curtsied prettily, for she was not at all high in the instep, and the fact that she was an earl's daughter and the guests merely a baron and his family bothered her not at all.

"Everyone is in the Gold Saloon," she announced, "but perhaps you would prefer to rest before you meet them."

"Not a rest after so short a journey," Lady Harmon assured her, "but perhaps a chance to remove the dust of the road." She had frequently made unfavourable comments upon the length of the trip, but she was not about to utter a complaint to the girl she was already seeing as her daughter's sister-in-law.

"Oh, of course; Hawkins will take your cases to your rooms and show your dresser where she is to go. I am happy that you did not bring a maid, Emily, for I have chosen Spence for you and I think you will like her." In fact, Emily had never had an abigail at the Hall and, Molly having been left in London to wed her young man, Hough had rather ungraciously received the information that she was to wait upon Miss Emily as well as Lady Harmon during the visit. "Dobbs," continued Lady Violet, "will you tell her ladyship that I shall bring the guests down when they have seen their rooms?"

"Very good, m'lady," Dobbs said stiffly and moved away, too well acquainted with Lady Violet's behaviour to see anything out of the common way in her taking over the servant's task of conducting the guests to their rooms.

A sharp nip upon the arm by Lady Harmon had prevented Emily from making her curtsy to this individual, who had appeared so grand that the girl had thought he must be the earl at least, if not the duke. As her parents moved ahead of her in the wake of the footman who bore their cases, there was no one to tell her not to curtsy to the solemn figure that stood beside the stairpost. Since it gave no indication of having seen her action and Lady Violet had made no introduction, she peered more closely and blushed in confusion as she realised that what she had greeted was not a guest but a mere suit of armour. When she tried to explain how she had made such an error, Lady Violet laughed gaily.

"You are quite right to show such respect," she said teasingly, "for that is all that remains of the founder of our house, Sir Edmund Leslie. Papa is named for him; he was a second son, and since that time the second Leslie son is always named Edmund. He—Sir Edmund, I mean, and not Papa, of course—was quite a favourite of Queen Elizabeth, as the story goes. Apparently, he was only one of many."

She linked her arm in Emily's, and they mounted the stairs together as she went on talking. "As a mark of her favour, he received this property—or a part of it, at least—at her hands and wished to name it in her honour. But there must have been any number of Queen's this and Queen's that by that time, and he wished something that would mark it as different from the others. In honour of her . . . unmarried state, he named it Maidencourt. I believe the allusion"—Emily misunderstood the word to be "illusion" and blushed at her friend's frank speech—"found great favour with Her Majesty. There was a Norman tower here and an abbey beside it—no longer in use, of course. Sir Edmund tore down everything but the tower and built his house against it, using the old stones. Throughout the years, the family has added to the house and grounds until we are as you see us now."

You mean, as I do *not* see you, Emily said to herself as they entered a bedroom. Even Lady Violet, dear as she had become in so short a time, seemed to have forgotten completely how impossible it was for her to see anything that was not directly before her eyes.

In truth, Lady Violet had entirely forgot the fact, for she was as feather-witted as she was charming. She had, however, felt an instant friendship with Emily and considered her one of the most beautiful girls she had met in London. She hoped that Emily was beautiful enough to distract Arthur from his pursuit of Lady Isobel Darcy, who, aside from having a *tendre* for their cousin, was much too old for Arthur.

36

Why, from the length of time she had been out, she must be five-and-twenty, at least—almost an old crone.

Why could not her idiotish brother see that there was not a chance for him with Lady Isobel, since it was clear that she had set her sights upon a duchess's coronet? But Arthur was making an absolute cod's head of himself over the woman and might well incur their cousin's wrath.

For all that Philip was the mildest of men in company, it did not seem that he had ever had much use for his cousin Arthur, and her ladyship shuddered to think what might happen if he lost his temper. She had heard that the duke exercised regularly while in London with some former fighters named Jackson and Cribb—at least, she thought those were the names.

Arthur might be—face it, he certainly was—a fool, but his sister was fond of him and hoped to be able to rescue him from the results of his foolishness. Emily would make a perfect wife for him, Lady Violet thought, unaware that her thoughts were running along the same path as those of Emily's mama.

"This is Spence, who will care for you," Lady Violet announced. "Spence, this is Miss Emily Harmon."

The vague shape which Emily took to be Spence bobbed a curtsy and, as Lady Violet sat upon her friend's bed and continued to chatter, moved about the room, pouring water so that Emily could wash and guiding her in the direction of the basin. From the young lady's clothes, she chose a gown of straw-coloured muslin, which was less in need of pressing than some of her other garments, and buttoned Emily into it, carefully tying the sash of deeper yellow silk and shaking out the vandyked flounce about its hem.

More observant than her mistress—because her little sister had the same mysterious difficulty in seeing—Spence realised that Miss Harmon would doubtless be in need of aid during her visit. As far as was in her power, the abigail determined to give her that aid.

When Lady Harmon, surprised and slightly resentful at

finding that no footman had been assigned to wait for the new arrivals and conduct them downstairs, puffed into her daughter's room to see if she was ready and to tell her that his lordship was being kept waiting, her usual scold was stopped by the sight of Lady Violet lounging on Emily's bed. Lady Harmon apologised for having interrupted her, but the young lady sprang to her feet and smoothed the skirts of her amber silk gown as she said, "Oh, no, you must not. My tongue runs like a fiddlestick, Arthur is forever telling me, and I fear he is right. It is I who should apologise to you for not coming to see if you were comfortable, since my mama is with the other guests. But I was so eager for a cose with Emily that I forgot everything else. And please, you must not call me Lady Violet here. I am just Violet to my friends. And we are friends, are we not? I feel that Emily and I might be sisters."

She slipped an arm about Emily's waist as she spoke, and Lady Harmon beamed upon the two of them, thinking what a pretty pair they made. And that speech about her ladyship feeling that they were sisters. . . . If the rest of the family welcomed Emily as did Lady Violet—she must remember that it was no longer necessary to call her "Lady"—her future was assured. Emily's future, she amended her thoughts.

The Gold Saloon seemed to be filled with people when they entered, but Violet, her arm still in Emily's—for which the girl was grateful—led them across the room to her parents and presented them. The earl and the countess, neither of whom was as fashionably dressed as the majority of their guests, greeted them without the slightest hint of hauteur, raising Lady Harmon's hopes still higher.

The earl, who would have much preferred being out among his precious roses, puttering about in his oldest clothes, hopefully questioned Lord Harmon to see if he might be a fellow enthusiast. While he was reluctant to disappoint his host, Lord Harmon had no interest in horticulture and would not pretend otherwise. Shaking his head sadly, the earl said, "No one else here cares for such things, either," and led him to a group of gentlemen who were busily decrying the latest moves of His Majesty's government. The countess meanwhile introduced Lady Harmon to several other ladies, then drew her down onto the sofa for a chat.

Being thus dismissed by the ladies, Violet again linked her arm in Emily's and led her to various groups of people, making introductions. There were several young men airily dismissed as "only friends of Arthur's; you need not mind them," which brought a protest—"Oh now, Vi, that is unfair!"—from one of them.

Next they reached a pair of fair young ladies whose chatter was as much alike as their appearance. "Laura Maugham and Marjorie Allenby." Even Violet seemed to think them so much alike that it was not necessary to distinguish between them. Looking toward the groups of elders, she added, "I shall present you to their parents later."

One lady stood out from the throng because of the vivid green of the gown she wore. If only she could continue to wear that colour, I would be able to recognise her, Emily thought, unaware that her wish might be realised. Green was the lady's favourite colour—especially the brighter hues, as they set off to perfection her milk white skin and masses of red-gold hair. They also matched the emerald pendant that nestled above the extreme décolletage of her gown. A gift from the gentleman to whose arm she clung, it was only the first of many emeralds she would own if her plans materialised.

"Lady Isobel Darcy," Violet said in a voice she barely managed to keep civil, adding in a much warmer tone, "and my cousin, the Duke of Durban."

So Mama had been wrong about that much, Emily told herself, making her curtsy as the gentleman bowed over her hand. The duke had come to the house party after all. She also recalled that Mama had said he was expected to offer for the Lady Isobel. Certainly he must have done so, for even she could see that the lady kept her white arm through the black-clad one of her escort. It seemed unlikely that a lady would cling to a gentleman in such a manner unless they were to be married.

Lady Isobel was rumoured to be a beauty of the first stare, and Emily wished that she might look at her closely to see what made her so beautiful, but felt that her ladyship would not like it if she did so. People frequently resented having another face peering closely at their own. It was only the ladies who resented this, she had noticed; gentlemen sometimes seemed to consider it an invitation, so Emily had quickly learnt not to approach them too closely, either.

About this gentleman she could tell nothing whatever, except that he wore a black coat and, she thought, a plain white waistcoat. It had seemed to her that he was fair-haired, but she could not be certain; his bow over her hand had been so brief, and he was so tall when he straightened. Perhaps his hair was white. The few dukes she had met were rather elderly men, several with a tendency to try to pinch her, thinking they should be excused for such behaviour because of their age. She was happy that *this* duke did not behave so, even if he was old.

Still, Mama had also said something about Durban setting up his nursery. In such a case, would he not have to be a fairly young man? Such matters were not customarily discussed in the presence of young ladies, and Emily began to blush fiercely at even thinking of them, causing the duke to look at her in surprise, for certainly nothing had been said at which the child might take offence.

She might have been displeased at Isobel's behaviour; her nod of acceptance had been curt in the extreme (in fact, Emily had not even seen it), and she had tugged at his arm, curtailing his bow. Isobel was not fond of ladies, especially young ones, but that should not have embarrassed the girl unless she was terribly shy.

He smiled broadly at Emily to compensate for Isobel's

rudeness and was still further surprised when his smile was not returned. It was his experience that young ladies—and others who were no longer young—were customarily impressed at receiving any attention from him. This was not entirely due to his rank and wealth; both his height and his handsome features would have made him stand out in any crowd.

The little Harmon—if that was what Violet had called her—was an odd child, thought the duke. He shrugged and turned back to listen to what Isobel was saying and to loosen gently the fingers that were grasping his sleeve until his perfectly fitting jacket was nearly pulled from his shoulder.

"My brother Arthur," Violet said next, "and Sir John Barham." Her voice was decidedly warm when she made this introduction. She must be very fond of her brother, Emily thought, much fonder than I am of George. Or was it the other gentleman whose presence gave her so much pleasure?

Making her curtsy to the pair, Emily wished that Violet had indicated which of the two was her brother. Her ladyship would have done so if she had remembered Emily's problem. To her, there was little resemblance between her brother and a man of the world who had passed his thirtieth birthday, but to Emily they seemed much alike. Both of them seemed to be clad in much brighter clothes than the duke—or indeed, any of the other gentlemen—and, as far as she could tell, either was dark enough to be Violet's brother.

One of the gentlemen hardly bothered to bow over her hand, but the other one held it and pressed his lips to it so fervently that Emily wished she could snatch it from his grasp. Still, if it *was* the viscount who was being so gallant, she would not wish to discourage him.

She discovered that she had been in error as to which gentleman was which several moments later when dinner was announced. The pale blur that must have been Violet's hand was being placed upon the sleeve of the gentleman who had kissed Emily's fingers, and Violet was saying to the other, "Arthur, Emily is to be your partner at dinner."

41

"But I had arranged—" the viscount began, then became aware that his mother's eye was fixed upon him from the far side of the room, and broke off what he had been about to say, muttering instead that he would be happy to be Emily's escort.

Violet was quite accustomed to her brother's sulks and paid no attention. Emily could not see the scowl that had accompanied his words, but she did not think he sounded as if he wished her company. Hearing him, she despaired of having the chance to obey her mama's orders and capture his interest. It seemed to her that the young man actually disliked her, although she could not understand why he should do so when they had only met.

She was mistaken in this. To the viscount, Miss Harmon did not matter one way or the other; he would have been unaware of her existence if his sister had not brought her to his attention, and he would have felt the same about any lady chosen to be his dinner partner—any except one. What angered him was that he had managed to slip into the dining room when Dobbs had finished directing the laying of the table and had herded the other servants from the room. There the viscount had changed the setting of the table so that he would be able to take in Lady Isobel. Now he found that someone—probably his brat of a sister, who delighted in making touble for him—had undone his plans and had saddled him with this chit.

Viscount Stearnes had only two ambitions, equally foolish in the eyes of those who knew him best. First, he aspired to be a Tulip of the Ton and had chosen Sir John Barham (who was something of a laughingstock to everyone but Arthur and Violet) as his model, aping the older man's extremely high shirt-points, heavily padded shoulders, gaudily embroidered waistcoats, and multitude of fobs. And second, he was determined to win the hand of Lady Isobel Darcy.

4

STEARNES WAS AWARE that the *on-dit* in London, and here as well, was that Isobel was determined to marry his cousin, but he had convinced himself that this was only because Philip had been careful to give her no opportunity to know him. Once he could find some way to speak to her—really speak to her; not merely the usual social chatter—he was certain that he could convince her that his love for her was much more sincere than Philip's.

In fact, he did not believe that Philip loved Isobel; he was merely thinking of marrying her because her lineage would make her a suitable duchess. The dear girl deserved better than that.

What can one expect of an old stick like Philip? he often asked himself. Never thinks of anything, I am sure, except his estates. How could he know anything about love—*real* love, such as I feel for Isobel?

Having led Emily to the table, he felt that he had done his duty toward her, and ignored her throughout the entire meal, sitting and gazing moodily up the table at Lady Isobel. She was flirting—actually flirting—and not only with Philip, who seemed to respond absently, but with the gentleman on her other side as well.

Dear Isobel, Arthur thought, she has such liveliness; it must be galling to her to be forced to accept old Philip, so it was no wonder that she behaved in such a way sometimes.

She would be a different person when he had the opportunity to demonstrate to her how very much he loved her.

He thought that his feeling was a secret from his adored one, but in common with all his family and friends, Isobel was quite aware of it. She was probably the first to have known of his ambitions in her direction, for Isobel was never blind to the attentions of any male. Doubtless, some ladies would have been pleased and touched at such devotion from a gentleman five years their junior; to her ladyship, Lord Stearnes was a ridiculous young puppy. Did he truly believe that there was anything he could give her which could compare with the things she really craved and which Durban could bring her—jewels and an imposing title?

Seated at the viscount's side, Emily wondered miserably how she was expected to do as her mama had ordered and fix the gentleman's interest. What could she do when he did not even address a single word to her and ignored her few tentative efforts to begin a conversation?

After all, she asked herself, what do I know that would be of interest to a gentleman?

The young man who was on her other side—she thought he was one of the viscount's friends, but did not know his name—did address several remarks to her in a hearty voice. His conversation, however, was limited to the two topics most important to him: horses and racing. Emily knew nothing of either, and his talk was filled with so many cant terms that he might as well have been speaking Greek.

Finding her company dull, he soon turned his interest to his other neighbour, who was equally ignorant, but who gushed replies and batted her eyelashes at him so that he preened himself with the thought that she found him an interesting fellow.

So Emily sat in isolation, hoping that she could manage to get through the dinner without any of the unfortunate accidents which frequently occurred to her. Her mama would never forgive her if she leaned down to see her plate, and the others—if they happened to be looking in her direction, which she doubted—would certainly think her odd. She must do the best she could. One piece of meat for which she had been searching with her fork did fly off her plate, but the footman stationed behind her chair deftly removed it before anyone had noticed. Later, he caught her wine glass, which she had set down upon the blade of her knife, in time to keep it from spilling its contents into her lap.

"A quiet-appearing little thing like that," he commented after dinner to one of his companions. "She looked all right, too. Who would have thought that she'd be foxed so early in the evening?"

"One thing you'll learn, my lad," the older man said, "when you've been in service as long as I have—you never can tell about Quality. I could tell you some tales that would curl your liver."

There was one person at the table who had noticed how Emily was being ignored by her dinner partner and who resolved to speak to Arthur about his lack of manners. The earl ought to be the one to do so, but it would be useless to mention the matter to him, for his principal concern was with a blight that appeared to be threatening one of his roses. And after all, the duke reminded himself, *he* was the head of the family. However, he was not in the habit of using the position to attempt to influence any of the other members of the family, and he doubted that Arthur would pay attention to anything that he said. Ten years ago Arthur had followed at his heels, hanging upon every word and flattered that a cousin six years his senior would condescend to notice him at all. Now it was Barham's habits that the viscount copied, and Durban could not think of a worse model than the slightly aging man of the town. A care-for-nobody, that was Barham, and Arthur was beginning to be nearly as bad. At least he had not yet begun to show any signs of wishing to ape Barham's rakish tendencies; the family could be happy about that, even if he was being such an idiot about Isobel.

Still, the duke resolved to speak to the boy about his duty to a guest, knowing that it would probably be a waste of his time to do so.

When the ladies arose to withdraw, Violet drew her mother aside, although she knew she might expect to receive a scold later for such a lack of manners. However, she felt that she could wait no longer to learn the countess's opinion of Emily, and confided her hopes that her new friend might serve to distract the viscount's attention from Lady Isobel.

"I hope that something may serve to do so, my dear, whether it is your friend or some other interest," the countess said doubtfully. "But one must not expect too much. You will learn that men are notoriously blind, and one cannot expect them to see what is best for them. This is why wives—and mothers as well—have such a difficult time. It is my belief that Arthur does not truly care for Isobel; he only thinks he does because she prefers his cousin. Or I think I should say that she prefers Durban's title. I wish that I need not have invited Isobel at this time until Arthur had a chance to outgrow his foolishness. But since Durban had agreed to be present, how could I not do so?"

Her daughter had heard all of this before and agreed with every word. "But what do you think of Emily?" she persisted.

"I have hardly had an opportunity to judge her," her mother reminded her, "but she seems to me to be a quiet, nice young lady. Bring her to me, and we shall have a talk. Now, we have neglected our friends far too long."

She moved on into the drawing room, apologising to the other ladies for making them wait, and Violet sped back to Emily, slipping an arm about her waist.

"My mama wishes to talk to you," she said, leading Emily away from the others to the countess's side.

Lady Montayne took Emily's hand to draw her down upon the sofa. Across the room, Lady Harmon, who had been disappointed not to be invited to occupy that important place, now smiled in satisfaction to see that it was her daughter who was being given the honour. Certainly that must be a good sign.

If his mother approves of Emily, there cannot be any doubt that Lord Stearnes will soon take an interest in her, she said to herself, and settled back in her chair, allowing the flood of gossip to flow over her, but barely hearing a word of it. She was wishing that she could be close enough to where Emily was seated with the countess so that she could speak up on her daughter's behalf if the girl should be overcome by shyness.

Prepared to be impressed with the countess's grandeur, Emily soon found that the timidity she naturally felt at meeting new people had melted away, for the older woman was all kindness to her. Lady Montayne could not fail to be aware of her own physical defects; she was possessed of a visage that all too often reminded others of the horses of which she was so fond. Emily did not know this, but it would not have mattered to her if she had known it, and the countess much preferred the girl's quiet deference to Isobel's scarcely veiled ridicule.

Her nephew, the countess thought, could deal with a vixen like Isobel; her son would never be able to do so. She considered that the family was fortunate that it was the duke's title Isobel was after. There would be no danger of having her for a daughter-in-law. She was beginning to share Violet's hope that Arthur might come to prefer someone like this engaging young girl.

Under the countess's pleasant questioning, Emily artlessly confided all about her home in Lincolnshire, thankful that she could describe it so much better now that she had been able to see it these past months. From there, the talk went to her London season and how nervous she had been during her presentation. Since all young ladies were nervous at such a time, the countess did not find this unusual, for Emily did not tell the reason for her near-panic, only saying how kind

Violet had been to her. Several times she caught herself upon the verge of mentioning her spectacles, but, remembering her mama's strictures upon the subject, she spoke of other things. The countess could not fail to notice the abrupt changes in the conversation, but thought little of them.

Girls of her age always have some little secrets to hug to their hearts, she said to herself, being able to recall—even after so long a time—at least one hopeless passion of her youth, fortunately soon outgrown. Doubtless there was some little flirtation while she was in London, harmless in itself, but meaning so much to her. Nothing, I am certain, that would prevent her from holding Arthur's interest—if we can ever stop him from making such a cake of himself over Isobel.

"Did you see any plays while you were in London?" she asked. "It seemed to me that while we were there, Violet was forever plaguing me to allow her to attend some play—and many of the ones presented were entirely ineligible for a young lady, in my opinion."

Perhaps she should not have said that last. A young lady anxious to remain in her good graces would naturally agree with her. Still, she thought that Emily was too naive to do other than tell the truth, so she believed her when she said, "No, your ladyship, I . . . I find that I do not care greatly for plays."

How could Emily explain that it would be useless for her to attend unless she was permitted to wear her forbidden spectacles? On the one occasion when she had been persuaded to go, she had spent the entire evening wondering what was happening upon the stage to make everyone laugh, and had begged off from going another time.

"And Violet tells me that you do not care to dance?"

Emily shook her head, and Lady Montayne looked thoughtful. No dancing and no playgoing; that seemed to indicate almost a Puritan state of mind. Such a girl would never do for Arthur. Still, while it was most suitable for a girl of her age, there was nothing bespeaking the Puritan about the gown Emily was wearing, nor about her conversation. It was more probable that, having grown up in the country, the child was merely more accustomed to a quiet life than girls like Violet, who had made frequent visits to London even before they were out. And after all, Arthur did not care to dance, and sneered at plays, so that would not be a problem.

Emily's quietness might be a very good thing. The countess did not consider that she was particularly straitlaced, but of late had found herself shocked by the revealing gowns and the all-too-free behaviour of many of the ladies of the ton, especially those of Lady Isobel's coterie. It was rumoured —and Lady Montayne was willing to believe it—that the young woman's actions were such as to have caused two gentlemen to sheer off just as it was thought they would be making her an offer and that, at five-and-twenty, she would definitely be left upon the shelf if she could not capture Durban.

Several of the young ladies of the party commented to one another upon the fact that the countess kept Emily at her side for such a length of time. They knew that Lady Montayne was notoriously kind-hearted; doubtless, she pitied the girl who knew no one here except Violet, although they would certainly have taken her into their company at once if permitted to do so.

"Poor thing," Marjorie Allenby remarked to Laura Maugham, but softly, so that her words would not reach Violet, standing a little apart from them at the moment, looking with satisfaction at her mother and her friend, who seemed to be pleased with one another. "Is the old lady really trying to make her feel at home? It looks more as if she is cross-questioning her."

"Still, she does not seem to be trying to get away."

"What can she do? You cannot tell the countess, 'I'd rather not be talking to you.' " Then, as the countess's daughter joined them, they began to chatter about other things, to touch their hair cautiously to see that every curl was in place, and to straighten their flounces when the gentlemen could be heard approaching.

Lady Isobel had thought that the duke's aunt really should be giving her more attention, as she was the ranking lady among the guests, but the conversation of ladies had always bored her, and she was waiting with impatience for the duke's arrival. As he entered the room, she went to him at once, linking her arm possessively in his.

She behaves as though she thought I might make a bolt, that gentleman thought with a touch of annoyance, but the lady's only motive was to warn others away.

When urged by some of the other gentlemen, especially Arthur, to play for them, she drew the duke with her to the spinet, begging him prettily to turn the pages of her music, causing his cousin—who had been hoping for that pleasant duty and could not know how willingly the duke would have relinquished it—to retreat with a scowl.

Her ladyship was an accomplished musician, and she rendered several lengthy sonatas to polite comment from some of her listeners. As soon as her last note was struck, she turned from the instrument, drawing the duke down to sit beside her so that she could talk to him intimately, and ignoring the others. The countess, who had little liking for music and less for the behaviour of her titled guest, asked, "Do you play the spinet, Miss Harmon?"

"Oh no," Emily exclaimed. "That is, yes, I do play . . . a little . . . but nothing so fine as *that*."

"Or the harp?" Lady Montayne persisted.

Emily shook her head, unhappily admitting that her accomplishments were limited.

"Good," the countess said heartily, her liking for the girl increasing every minute. "I loathe people who are forever displaying their talents, especially when those talents are so meagre. And I fear that they frequently are. Oh dear, now we shall be forced to listen to Marjorie Allenby sing."

That young lady, yielding to very little urging, approached

the spinet, struck several patently unrelated chords, and began her first song. Her voice was thin, but not entirely unmusical, and if it wandered about now and then searching for the proper note, the search was eventually successful—in most cases.

Her performance was no better and no worse than that of most of her contemporaries, but her repertoire was a large one. She would happily have regaled her audience with all of it, but at the end of her third song the countess signaled to the butler, who had been hovering in the doorway for several minutes. Aware of his mistress's opinion of amateur musicians, Dobbs had everything arranged so that the tea tray was brought in at once, marking the end of the concert.

As the countess poured, Violet accepted several cups of tea from her hands and took them to some of the guests. When she had moved away, Lady Montayne, thinking that the action would demonstrate to everyone her distinct approval of the young lady, said to Emily, ''My dear, will you be kind enough to take these to Lady Isobel and the duke?''

''Oh, I cannot,'' Emily demurred, but the countess had been expecting a polite protest and merely pressed the cups into her hands.

Unless she could confess the reason for her reluctance —and her mama would be very angry with her if she did so —Emily had no choice but to obey her hostess's wishes. Fortunately, Lady Isobel's vivid green gown was like a beacon on the far side of the room and, fixing her eyes upon it, Emily went carefully in that direction, hoping that she was holding the cups upright and not spilling any tea upon the carpet.

She skirted a large blur, which was actually a group of gentlemen who were standing near the sofa upon which the duke and Lady Isobel were seated. Since their discussion was about the results of the last election, tempers were running high, and one of the gentlemen was emphasising his arguments with angry gestures of his cane. It slipped from his grasp and fell directly in Emily's path.

Her foot came down upon it and, overbalanced, she pitched forward. One cup of tea splashed the sofa, barely missing the duke's impeccable evening jacket. The contents of the other went straight down the front of Lady Isobel's gown.

The tea was very hot, so there was pain mingled with rage in the scream her ladyship uttered as she sprang to her feet.

"You did that purposely," she shrieked at Emily, who was aware that there had been one of her usual mishaps, but had not been able to see where the tea had gone. "You—you little—" sputtered Lady Isobel, who, forgetting her intention of always behaving beautifully until she had caught the duke, slapped the girl so hard that she staggered and the empty teacups slipped from her fingers.

Emily felt an arm go about her shoulders, steadying her, and heard a gentleman's voice saying, "Do not be so harsh with the child, Isobel. It was an accident; it could have happened to anyone. General Allenby dropped his cane—"

"She should have stepped over it. Anyone but a complete fool would have known that it would roll beneath her feet," her ladyship raged, then burst into tears and ran from the room. The viscount, pausing only to cast an angry glance in the direction of Emily—seen by everyone except the one for whom it was intended—dashed after Lady Isobel to calm her, only to have her bedroom door slammed almost upon his nose.

In the drawing room, the duke still supported Emily, who was also in tears and saying half-hysterically, "I'm sorry— I'm sorry—I did not see—"

"Of course you did not," the gentleman was saying in sympathetic tones. "It was no more than an accident, so do not let it overset you. Lady Isobel will forget what happened, I can assure you. After all, what is a gown to her?"

He was not so certain that Isobel would forget, but, if necessary, he would convince her to pretend that she had done. It would be unfortunate if the child's visit were to be spoilt by this mishap.

Trembling so that she was still grateful for the strength of an arm about her, Emily was on the verge of confessing her inability to see any obstacle—or much of anything else, for that matter—when a sharp nip upon her arm told her that her mama had come up on her other side and that it would be best for her to remain silent about her affliction. Lady Harmon's arm was about her daughter, drawing her away from the duke as she said, "Your Grace is much too kind, coming to the aid of my little girl, but I fear all of this has been too great an ordeal for her. I think it would be best if we should withdraw, if you will permit it."

"Certainly," Durban said politely, releasing Emily and moving away to join the conversation of the group of gentlemen who had been—unintentionally—the cause of the accident. He was not aware of the curtsy Emily made, having been nearly pushed into it by her mama as she still found it difficult to think clearly.

With the briefest of excuses to the countess, and brushing aside her expression of sympathy, Lady Harmon drew Emily out of the room and hurried her up the stairs to her bedroom. Curtly dismissing the waiting Spence, she scarcely gave the abigail time to close the door behind her before beginning to berate the girl for her lack of conduct.

Emily was still shaking from fear and from the result of Lady Isobel's blow. All of her tearful protestations that the entire thing had been an accident did nothing to halt her mama's tirade.

"Of all the people present, you must throw tea on Lady Isobel," she said angrily, making Emily aware for the first time exactly what had happened. "An earl's daughter and the future Duchess of Durban. And it was only by good fortune that you missed drenching the duke as well. Durban may have been polite enough to pretend that nothing was

53

amiss, but it will be wonderful if we are not to receive a hint that we are no longer wanted here. I shall go down and do what I may to apologise to the countess." She paused at the door to add, "How you can expect to find any gentleman who will offer for you if you continue to behave in so *gauche* a fashion, I cannot understand."

= 5 =

THE MOMENT THAT she heard the door close behind Lady
Harmon, Spence, who had retreated no farther than the
turning of the hall, hastened back to Emily's room to find
the girl lying face down upon her bed, sobbing bitterly.

"There, miss," the woman began soothingly, patting
Emily's shoulder, then sitting on the side of the bed and
gathering her up in comforting arms. It was not her place to
behave in such a fashion with a guest, but she thought
angrily that this was what her ladyship had ought to be
doing, instead of giving her daughter a bear-garden jaw for
something she likely couldn't help. She saw the red mark on
Emily's face and wondered if the woman had actually struck
the girl. Shameful if she had done anything of the sort.
"Surely it cannot be as bad as all that. You will be sick if you
keep on in this way."

"It would be the best thing I could do," Emily said with a
hiccup. "In that case, I would not have to see any of them
again."

Nonetheless, the soothing words and gestures began to
have their effect, and before long Emily was coaxed into
allowing the abigail to bring her a damp cloth to wipe away
all signs of her tears and then to hold it against the bruise on
her cheek to ease its pain. Under Spence's sympathetic eyes,
she found herself telling all about the evening's disaster and
its cause.

Spence was not surprised to learn that Lady Isobel should

behave in such a manner, for the servants had their own opinions about *that* lady; but she thought it best not to say so.

"Yes, miss," she said instead, "I could tell that about you at once. My little sis's just the same—forever running into things and falling over something and saying she cannot see it."

The doctor had told Emily when he was fitting her for her spectacles that she was not the only young person who was so afflicted. Until that time, she had thought that only old people needed spectacles, and she had found his words difficult to believe. This was the first time she had spoken to anyone who understood.

Emboldened by the knowledge that there was at least one other girl who was in the same condition as she, she confided about the spectacles and how her papa had been persuaded to get them for her. Taking them from her reticule, she passed them to Spence, who examined them wonderingly, tried holding them up before her own eyes, but put them aside quickly, saying, "Oh, they make my eyes feel all swimmy, and I cannot see a thing through them. I do not see how you can bear to wear them. Wouldn't they make it harder for you to see instead of better?"

"No, they are great help—truly. I cannot explain it, of course, for I could not understand half the things the doctor said to me, but my eyes are not like yours. When I wear them, I can see all sorts of things I never knew about before."

As Spence, still doubtful that anything which so hurt her eyes could do otherwise when another wore them, shook her head, Emily placed the spectacles upon her own nose and said, "Now I can tell just how you look. I could not before. You were just a blur to me; everyone is. Perhaps spectacles such as these would be of help to your little sister. Why do you not tell your parents about them?"

"Oh no, my pa would never agree to such things for

Sukey; he'd say we'd never be able to get her married, and he'd be right. I can see now why your lady mother don't want you to be wearing them. Everyone would think you look . . . well, queer.''

"I suppose you are right," Emily said sadly, taking off the spectacles and placing them upon the dressing table. "At least, I know my mama feels just that way about them. What does it matter if I cannot see well, as long as I *look* well?''

She allowed the abigail to help her prepare for bed, certain that she would never be able to sleep after what had occurred, but so exhausted by the emotions of the evening that she had scarcely begun to think how she might apologise to Lady Isobel before she fell sound asleep.

Most of the members of the house party had left the drawing room when Lady Harmon came downstairs. Should her first apology be made to the duke or to her hostess? Durban was the most important member of the party, of course, but as he was deep in conversation with several gentlemen, she went to the countess and began to asperse her daughter's maladroitness. Lady Montayne put up a hand to stop her and said, "Do not refine too much upon it, I beg of you. Such a thing might easily have happened to anyone. The general is forever flinging his cane about—especially when he is arguing about politics, which he will do, despite anything a hostess can do to prevent it. I have often feared that someone will be injured by it, so it is fortunate that nothing worse occurred. He might have struck your daughter instead of merely tossing it into her path.''

Lady Harmon's protest that Emily should have managed to avoid the obstacle was waved aside.

"As for Isobel's outburst, it is my opinion that the girl has the manners of a fishwife. Where she gets them I cannot understand, for her mother is a delightful woman. It is a disturbing thought that she may soon be my niece; despite her bloodlines, I dislike to think of the position she will occupy if

Durban does marry her. Still, my nephew is of an age to make his own decisions, and I must only be thankful that Isobel wants him and not my son. Come, sit here with me, Lady Harmon, and let us enjoy a cup of tea while we talk. Aside from her little *contretemps*, I confess that I found your daughter a charming girl.''

Lady Harmon beamed and complied, not in the least displeased by the fact that the countess was at least as garrulous as her daughter. She was left little opportunity to speak, but as she agreed with her hostess on every point, this did not matter. By the time they were prepared to retire to their bedrooms, she and Lady Montayne were so much in accord that she thought once that she might look in upon Emily and tell her that she had been forgiven and that there would be no need for them to cut short their visit.

Then she shook her head and went along to her own room, determined to let the girl worry for a night that her behaviour had jeopardised her future. Perhaps that would make her watch her conduct more carefully in the days to come, she thought, quite unaware that the evening's events had been driven completely out of Emily's mind by the more exciting discovery that she was not the only girl with a problem in seeing.

Memory of her catastrophe returned in full force when she awoke, and even Spence's assurance that she looked her prettiest in one of her new gowns—a celestial blue muslin sprigged with white flowers and with a matching band of blue threaded through her curls—did little to help.

"I only wish that I did not have to see any of them," she complained. "Or I should say to let them see me, for I will not be able to see them. I am certain that they will all be watching me, wondering what I might do next."

It was Spence's opinion that most of the Quality thought only of what was happening at the moment—if they thought at all, which she often doubted—and she said bracingly,

"Oh no, miss; you will find that they have put that out of their minds entirely."

Emily began to think that Spence had been right, for everyone at the breakfast table welcomed her, and no word was said about the evening before. Violet and her friends drew Emily down to a seat near them as the countess wished her a good morning. The girl answered the questions about what she wished to eat and was enjoying their chatter, most of it nonsensical, but she looked up in apprehension as a late arrival entered the room, one whom even she could not fail to recognise.

Lady Isobel's rage had given way to thoughtfulness soon after she had fled to her room, and she had worried for some hours that her display of temper might have given Durban a disgust of her. The duke was quite the most important catch of the season, and her ladyship had already had far too many unsuccessful seasons at her back. She was in no position to permit this chance to escape her.

She was quite aware that, having at last decided that it was time he married, Durban had looked over the field and had come to the conclusion that her lineage made her the best choice for his duchess. There was no more love on his part than on hers, but Lady Isobel, too, considered that love was an emotion fit only for servants and shopgirls. She was determined to marry the duke, and nothing must occur to interfere with her plans.

Dressed in a riding habit of her favourite emerald green, she entered the breakfast room to see her quarry seated beside his aunt, so she made her way to the countess's side, saying penitently, "My dear Lady Montayne, I do hope that you can bring yourself to forgive me for my behaviour of last evening. I fear that I was so overset that I completely forgot myself and acted somewhat outrageously; but the shock of having a cup of scalding tea thrown at one must be blamed. Please say that you understand."

"I understand perfectly, Isobel," the countess said drily,

hoping that her nephew would also understand that the scene was being played entirely for his benefit; that Isobel could not care less about the opinion of his aunt. "But I think the one who really should receive your apology is Emily."

Emily! So the countess had already progressed to the point where she called the bungling little fool by her first name. And to suggest that *she* should apologise when it was this Emily who had been the cause of all the trouble. She looked out of the corner of her eye at the duke. He was smiling, but there was something in his expression that made her certain that he agreed with his aunt. Forcing a smile which in no way matched her inner feelings, she moved around the table toward Emily.

Seeing the bright green figure approaching, Emily arose, so nervous she might make another mistake that she nearly overturned her chair. She caught at it, but a footman had already set it upright, so she bruised her hand upon its back. Curtsying, she stammered, "I h-hope that you will forgive me, Lady Isobel. I truly did not mean to spill the tea on you."

"Of course you did not, child. I realised almost at once that it was an accident," Lady Isobel said, hoping that Durban was aware of how generous she was being to the brat. It would do much to counteract any unpleasant impression last evening's behaviour might have given him. "But you cannot blame me for being just a tiny bit overset at the time, can you?"

"Oh, no, no," Emily said nervously, happy that nothing more was to be made of the incident. Apparently, it had not been as bad as her mama had feared. However, she thought that Lady Isobel must have been more than slightly over-wrought to have struck her with such force. Her jaw still ached from the blow. "And I am sorry that your beautiful gown was spoilt."

"Oh, I have other gowns," her ladyship said airily, as if the loss was not important—which was far from being true. Lady Isobel's fortunes were at a low ebb, in fact. Even her family name was no longer enough to keep her dressmaker from sending unpleasant demands for her money. Only a definite engagement would be enough to satisfy the woman that payments would be forthcoming soon. This made it all the more imperative that she should bring the duke up to scratch as quickly as possible—before the party was over if it could be arranged. Still, she could not resist giving one last little stab.

"And I was not hurt . . . very much."

Ignoring the dismayed expression these words brought to the face of the younger girl—for it had not occurred to Emily that her ladyship might have been hurt by the tea—Lady Isobel, with the feeling that she had accomplished her task of soothing the duke, returned to his side and said coaxingly, "Durban, you did promise to take me for a nice gallop this morning. Have you not finished your breakfast yet?"

"In a moment, my dear," he said, presenting his cup to the waiting footman. When it had been refilled with coffee, his grace proceeded to sip it in a leisurely manner.

He had understood Isobel's motive for apologising to his Aunt Miranda as easily as the countess had done and had not been impressed by the performance. He was aware that she had not apologised to the little Harmon girl, despite the countess's suggestion that she should do so. Still, she and the child appeared to be on better terms now.

However, it would do no harm to show Isobel that she was not yet entirely back in his good graces. There were moments of late—and they were becoming more frequent—when her possessiveness grated upon his sensibilities. After all, he had not offered for her yet, so she had no right to behave as if he belonged to her.

Several minutes later, he pushed back his chair, excusing

himself to the countess, and went out. Seemingly unabashed by his treatment of her, Lady Isobel clung to his arm and pressed herself against him as they left. Violet uttered a deep sigh of relief, which earned her a glare from her brother before he, too, left the room, wondering how he could rescue Isobel from Philip's bad temper. Although no one else made a comment, the atmosphere about the breakfast table had certainly lightened with Lady Isobel's departure.

The young ladies had been discussing plans to go into the village and prowl about the various shops, although none of them had any expectation of finding merchandise worth the purchasing, for what could the village offer that could not be bettered in the London shops? Still, being female, they could not bear to think of any shop remaining unexplored, and it should prove an amusing way to spend the morning hours.

The others drew Emily into their conversation and, happy to be free from the worry about last evening's accident, she soon found herself along with them in the dogcart, which Violet drove. Neither the earl nor the countess thought it necessary for a groom to accompany them, for the village lay only a short distance beyond the extensive grounds of Maidencourt. It would not have been the proper thing in London, but here in the country they would be safe enough. Violet was accustomed to such freedom at home, since she knew all of their neighbours and had been allowed to run to the village whenever she liked. To travel unescorted, however, made the others feel especially daring.

Emily knew which of her companions was Violet, as she was the only one with black hair, but she was uncertain which of the fair-haired girls was Marjorie Allenby and which was Laura Maugham. Still, she remembered that the countess had said it was Marjorie who had sung last evening. Looking somewhere between the two vague shapes, she said somewhat mendaciously how much she had enjoyed the singing.

Marjorie tittered and thanked her, and was eager to explain that she would be able to offer them many more of her songs, for she knew at least a dozen more.

"A few of them," she admitted with another giggle, "are just slightly naughty, I fear, for my brother taught them to me." She was about to regale them with one of those songs when Laura interrupted.

"*I* should be happy to do my part in the entertaining this evening if only I had my harp. But Papa said that it would mean bringing another carriage, since it would not fit in with all our boxes, so he forbade me to bring it. He said that Mama and I already had packed far too many things for so short a visit; you know how gentlemen are when they have grown too old to be interested in clothes. But I should like to play for you. Do you have a harp which I might use, Violet?"

"No, Mama never wished me to learn."

Emily bit her lip to keep from smiling, for she remembered Lady Montayne's opinion of such exhibitions. In fact, she was certain that the countess disliked any type of entertainment by untrained young ladies, and she wondered if Laura's papa might not share that dislike.

"Do you sing?" one of the girls asked, and Emily, feeling certain that the question must have been meant for her, as the others must know one another's talents, said quickly, "I fear I cannot—not well, at any rate." At least she could please the countess, if not Lady Harmon, by doing nothing. "I do play the spinet—a little—but I should not dare to try after hearing Lady Isobel last evening."

"Yes, I thought that she would never be finished with pounding away, and a performance such as that is enough to make anyone decide *not* to copy her," Violet said, unwilling to admit that anything about the older woman was admirable.

Emily started a protest, for she had thought Lady Isobel's performance had been fine indeed, but her friend had already turned the conversation to a topic much more interesting to her: what they might expect to find in the village, which they were now entering. It was a small place, with the road running through its center and two short lanes at right angles.

Because of the needs of their other guests, it had not occurred to either the earl or the countess that this was marketing day, or they would have forbidden the outing; at such times, the village was customarily full of farmers and their stock. Today, however, it was quiet for some unexplainable reason. The young ladies spent more than two hours wandering in and out of the few shops, examining materials, trying on every bonnet that the local milliner had to offer, and giggling over gowns that were outmoded by London standards.

They were watched more or less tolerantly by the townspeople, out of respect for Violet's parents, who, everyone knew, would send along a footman in a day or two to pay for any damage to goods or to the storekeepers' feelings. Such outings by the young lady's guests had proven a good source of income to the village, although they seldom made any purchases.

Emily laughed whenever the others did, unable—unless the coversation told her—to know what amused them so greatly, but pleased to be one of the group. She was only dissuaded from purchasing a bonnet decorated with a quantity of coquelicot plumes, which the milliner had mistakenly thought would appeal to a certain "lady" of the town, by Violet's telling her that she would look exactly like Harriette Wilson if she wore it.

"In fact, I saw her in the park one day during the season, and she had one exactly like that," she laughed.

Emily's cheeks grew as bright as the plumes, and she dropped the bonnet as if it had burnt her fingers. Gently reared young ladies were not supposed to be aware of the existence of the notorious courtesan and persons of her kind, but how could they avoid the knowledge when the creatures displayed themselves regularly in the park in finery and carriages paid for by their "protectors"? Still, it would take a very daring lady to copy any of their styles.

Forcing a smile, Emily said, "In that case, I had best not buy it. What would everyone think of me?"

"Perhaps they would think that you were planning to go 'on the strut,'" suggested one of the blond girls, causing all four of them to dissolve in giggles at such an unlikely happening. The giggles erupted again on the way home each time one of them wondered aloud who in the village might buy such headwear and suggested such names as that of the squire's lady or the vicar's wife. At these last, their mirth almost overcame them entirely. Emily could not remember when she had had so much enjoyment—foolish as most of it might be—with girls of her own age. And not one of them suspected that she could not see as well as they.

They had left the village in the opposite direction from the way they had come, meaning to circle around to strike the road to Maidencourt a bit later. A number of townspeople were moving along the road, and they soon discovered the reason. Violet drew the bay gelding to a halt while she and two of her friends gazed at the colourful sight in the meadow.

"That is why they were not in town—the farmers, I mean. They have brought their produce here, and their livestock as well."

"A fair," Marjorie exclaimed. "I wonder that no one told us about it. Let us go and see it."

"Do you think we should?" Laura asked, and the other fair-haired girl giggled again.

"Of course we should not. It would not be an adventure if no one minded that we attend."

"We really ought not to be here at all, and certainly not without an escort," Violet said, but Marjorie was tugging at her arm, so she turned the dogcart into the meadow where other vehicles had been left.

"As long as there are the four of us, nothing can happen,"

Marjorie was urging. "And besides, if we only stay awhile, no one will know."

Although she was as eager to see the fair as her friends, Violet had a reason for hesitating. The other young ladies were strangers to the area, but there was a chance that she might be recognised by someone in the crowd that was pushing between the stalls. Still, it did not seem likely that any of her friends would be brushing elbows with the townsfolk, and she doubted that the shopkeepers or country people would feel called upon to tell her parents.

As she climbed down from the dogcart, still wondering if it might not be wiser to return home at once, an urchin ran up, offering to watch the vehicle for a penny. Feeling reckless, Violet agreed, and the four girls started off, arms linked, to view the wonders of the fair.

They halted outside a tent covered with strange markings, listening to the man who extolled the unusual powers of the gypsy fortune teller inside; then, with great daring, each of them took her turn at having her palm read. This was something that would not have been permitted if they had come with an escort, and they were not disappointed when they compared notes and found that the crone had predicted identical futures for them—good fortune, long journeys, and a handsome stranger for each.

Emily felt that if the old woman had any powers, she would have mentioned her—Emily's—inability to see. Did that mean that none of the other things she foretold were true, or was it perhaps that the seeress's mind operated on so high a plane that such physical handicaps counted for nothing?

"She made one mistake, of course," Violet said, sucking upon a sweet like a child. "There will not be any handsome stranger for me. I have already found my gentleman, and since I know he is true to me, I want no other."

"Sir John?" one of her friends asked, and her ladyship nodded happily. Emily could not see the nod, but she remembered how warm her friend's voice had been when she had introduced the gentleman. She also recalled, however, how fervently Sir John had kissed her own hand, and was not surprised when Laura said, "But, Violet, I . . . I have heard that Sir John is something of a rake." A "loose fish" had been the term her brother had used to describe the baronet, but she would not repeat that to Violet. Much as she respected Jack's judgement, it *might* not be true. "Will not your parents object to him?"

"Oh, I am certain that they will—at first. They think that I am too young to be serious about marrying anyone yet. And I know that people have said some things about John—which I do not believe. Of course, he *is* a little older."

Old enough to be your father, thought the two who had seen him, but they did not say so. Older gentlemen could sometimes be quite fascinating.

"Then how—"

"I can bring them around, I am certain of that, once they come to see how very much I love John and how he loves me. But you must not say anything—not at present. You see—"

"You mean, he has not spoken to your father?"

"I do not think that he has, or I certainly should have been told of it. He has not yet said anything to me—about marriage, I mean, although he has shown me in so many ways that he cares for me—and I feel certain that he *will* speak to me before he sees my papa, even if it is not the proper thing to do."

"Oh, I do not think that Sir John concerns himself greatly with what is *proper*," Marjorie said, and she and Laura went off into another fit of giggles.

Emily told herself that the other girls were right about the gentleman, or it might be that she was refining too much upon the manner in which Sir John had kissed her hand. That had not seemed at all the proper sort of behaviour for one who was courting another, but she was forced to admit that a single season had certainly not made her adept at the types of flirtation that went on among the members of the ton. How could it have done when she could not see how they acted?

Violet was inclined to take exception to the unflattering comment about the gentleman who filled all her waking and dreaming thoughts; at least, she was not aware of thinking of such other things as parties and gowns. A quarrel might have sprung up among the friends, but they were interrupted by a number of shouts and squeals.

A small pig, liberally coated with grease, came tearing along the pathway with half a dozen young men bent upon catching it. They caromed into the four young ladies, separating them, then ran on, followed by a large portion of the crowd eager to see the finish of the contest.

Caught up in the push of the crowd, Emily was nearly swept off her feet and only remained upright by allowing herself to be carried along with them for some moments. Then the others pushed past her, leaving her standing alone

=== 6 ===

WHERE WERE THE other girls by this time? Had they been brought along as she had, or had they been left behind? Emily had no idea of how far she had been carried, nor in which direction, as the crowd had surged this way and that, following the animal's erratic path. Would her friends not call out to her if they were nearby and could see her?

"If only I had thought to bring my spectacles," she said aloud, past caring whether anyone might be near enough to overhear her and to learn her disgraceful secret.

At least it was disgraceful in her mama's eyes, Emily knew, and it seemed that Spence felt the same, although perhaps she did not think it quite so much disgraceful as merely unfortunate.

Of course, there had been no way of foreseeing that anything such as this would happen, and Lady Harmon would never have let her live it down if she had dared to wear them while riding or shopping with her friends. So the spectacles lay upon the dressing table in her room at Maiden-court, useless to her now.

Without them, she had not the slightest idea of which way she should go to find the other girls, but surely the fair could not be so *very* large. If she could find her way back to the fortune teller's tent, she believed that she would be able to recognise it, for she had stood near enough to it that she could make out some of the strange symbols it bore.

The others would certainly come that way as they looked

for her. For an instant, panic seized her at the thought that they might leave her, thinking she could find her way home alone. She fought it down; she did not know the other girls well enough to know what they would do, but Violet would never desert her.

She began to walk cautiously in what she hoped was the right direction, a hand outstretched to prevent herself from running into obstacles. She gasped as a hand that was much too large to belong to one of the girls fastened itself about her wrist.

"Alone, pretty?" The voice was slurred, and the reek of spirits almost overwhelmed Emily as he drew her toward him. "We can't have that, now can we? This is a time for enjoyment, and bein' alone's no fun, I can tell you. Come along with me and I'll buy you all the gauds you c'd fancy."

Emily's fright was so intense that she could do no more than squeak as she wrenched her arm from his grasp and rushed off, so that she plunged against a stall, sending unseen goods clattering to the earth while their owner swore at her for her clumsiness. Making her way around the stall, she collided with several merrymakers, who looked at her curiously, wondering if she might be foxed or demented, but who made no move to stop her.

The man who had accosted her looked after her as she darted first into one obstacle, then another. He thought at first that he would go after her, for she was a pretty little thing. Then he shrugged his shoulders and went on his way. After all, there were plenty of females here today who would not scorn his offer of presents, so why should he worry about this one? Still, he wondered why she should be roaming about the fair alone if it were not trade she was seeking. Unless she was some poor half-witted creature; and in such a case he wanted nothing to do with her.

Emily's companions had also been separated by the crowd, but none had been carried so far away as she. They had not time to be truly frightened at the idea of being alone before they had found one another. When they looked about for Emily, however, she was nowhere to be seen.

"We must find her," Violet cried. "And at once. If we are very late in arriving home, there are certain to be questions."

"And I dread to think what would be said if it is learnt that we had been here alone," Laura said with a shudder, and Marjorie, conveniently forgetting that she had suggested this "adventure," added, "I would not be surprised if your mama suggested that we ought not to stay at Maidencourt any longer—and what would my parents say if I was sent home in disgrace? We *must* find her. But which way ought we to go?"

"Perhaps we would find her more quickly if each of us went in a different direction. We could meet back here from time to time," Laura suggested, but the others vetoed that idea at once.

"No. If any of us should be recognised while we were going about alone, it would be far worse than if we are all seen together," Violet told her.

"And who knows what might happen to any one of us if the others were not nearby?" added Marjorie.

The truth of these words was proven several times as they searched the various paths, for, although they were invited more than once to join one of the groups of rather tipsy males who prowled the fair, their number prevented them from being forced to go, as might have happened if one of them had been alone. And what about Emily, each wondered but dared not ask the others; could she discourage such invitations?

They started in the direction that they supposed Emily had been driven by the crowd, but in her panic at having been accosted by the drunken stranger, the girl had run off in a different direction entirely. The cries of the crowd following the pig-chasers seemed to come from several sides, so they could not follow that. They had almost despaired of finding their friend when they spied her some distance ahead and moving away from them. Eager to get her and escape from the fair, Laura and Marjorie started after her, but Violet, crying "Wait!", caught each of them by the arm and drew them into the shelter of a nearby stall.

"Why did you do that?" Laura asked indignantly. "We almost had her; now we are sure to lose her again."

"You mean that you did not see?"

"See what?" Laura asked while Marjorie shook her head. Violet pointed in the direction Emily was taking and caught the others again, signalling them to be silent. The duke was strolling in their direction, Lady Isobel clinging to his arm and the viscount trailing them. Emily was heading directly toward them, but they had not yet seen her.

"What are we to do?" Laura asked as they drew quickly out of sight. "How can we help her?"

"There is no way that we can," Marjorie replied. "She is certain to be caught, and it would be best if we were to slip away before we are seen as well."

"Perhaps not," Violet exclaimed, loath to desert her friend. "The two of you stay here."

Dodging behind the stalls as skillfully as if she were an urchin bent on escaping the law instead of a young lady of Quality, she peered out once more to see that Lady Isobel had drawn the duke's attention to some display or other—ridiculing it, if her expression could be read aright. For a moment, both of them turned away and, thankful for such good fortune, Violet sped out of her hiding place, grasped Emily by the arm, and tugged her toward safety.

Emily shrieked as the hand caught her, remembering the man who had accosted her earlier and thinking he had found her again. The clamour of the crowd, however, was enough to muffle the sound; and Violet's voice in her ear, sternly ordering her to be silent, was recognised and obeyed. Emily permitted herself to be hurried away to the spot where the other girls were awaiting them.

"Where have you been all this time?" one of the girls

asked accusingly, and Emily felt that she had to justify her absence, even if it had not been of her doing.

"Trying to find you. The crowd carried me off, and I lost my way." What use would it be to tell them that she could not have seen which way they had gone even if there had been time to do so?

"What does it matter?" Violet asked. "We were separated, too, for a time; it only took a bit longer to find Emily. Now we are together again, and if we can get home unseen—or at least get to the road before we are recognised —we shall have no trouble."

There were no further mishaps along the way, but it was not thought that the young ladies would get off scot-free from their "adventure." Except for Emily, who had not seen her danger, they had been badly frightened at the narrowness of their escape from being seen by the duke and Lady Isobel, and Emily still feared that someone would find out about the man who had accosted her and would feel that it had been her fault for not being with the others.

It was so long past the luncheon hour when they returned that it was natural they would be questioned as to the reason for the delay. Violet's explanation that they had been driving about the countryside was received with some scepticism, but she apologised so prettily for having neglected the other guests that the four of them were let off with only a slight scold for their thoughtlessness. All of them, especially her young ladyship, who should have been responsible for the others, were warned, however, that while unescorted trips to the village might be permitted, it was far from wise for young ladies to wander abroad without even a groom in attendance.

Neither Mrs. Allenby nor Mrs. Maugham blamed their daughters overmuch, preferring to think that the fault lay with Lady Violet. They agreed that the earl and the countess were much too lax in the supervision of their daughter; but no harm had been done since they were in the country and no one of importance could have seen their unescorted drive. Also, it was scarcely good form to criticise one's hosts— especially when those hosts were important peers.

Lady Harmon would have liked to blame Emily for wasting so much time with other young ladies instead of pursuing the viscount. Even her questioning—which had been persistent enough to raise eyebrows among any but the best-trained servants—had failed to discover where Lord Stearnes had been spending his day, however, so she doubted if Emily could have done any better. Also, one of the young ladies *had* been Lord Stearnes's sister, so she contented herself with saying, "Remember, Emily, that we shall be here only a short time. You must exert yourself to attach Lord Stearnes. That is our reason for being here."

My reason was only to visit a friend, Emily answered, but only to herself. Her mama would have given her a severe scold, both for her impudence and for the fact that she must never forget that a young lady's first duty was to find a husband.

Marjorie was inclined to think that only Emily should have been blamed for the delay, but the others convinced her that there was no way that could have been done without confessing where they had spent their time, and that it was they, rather than Emily, who had wished to attend the fair. Laura reminded Marjorie that *hers* had been the original suggestion that they stop, so any blame should be hers, and the two would have begun to quarrel had not Violet made peace by declaring, "No, none of us can be blamed for what happened. The true fault lies with those boys who were chasing the pig, and with all the others who came between us and drove us apart. And since we were not seen by anyone who knew us, no harm was done."

Violet did not know that she was not entirely correct in this. They had not been seen, it was true, by either the duke or Lady Isobel. If they had been, it was unlikely that Durban would have reported the escapade to his aunt and uncle, for he was fond of Violet, but he would most certainly have read the four of them a stern lecture upon the impropriety of wandering about the fair alone.

Violet did not doubt that if Lady Isobel had seen them, *she* would have told on them at once. It would have been partly for spite, as Violet had guessed—for Isobel was quite aware of the younger girl's dislike of her and returned it—and partly because she would have felt that Durban would be favourably impressed by her concern for his relative's welfare.

It was the viscount who had observed his sister's dash from her hiding place and the return to it with Emily in tow. He had been following the duke and Lady Isobel about the fair for the better part of an hour, listening to her scornful remarks about the various displays and sneering at them in his turn, although on some other occasion a number of them would have held his interest. Having missed her latest comment to his cousin, he had not turned away when they did; thus it was that he had seen his sister and the other girl.

He was not concerned, however, with Violet's escapades. As for her friends, all of them several years younger than he, they were dismissed by him as "whey-faced brats," unworthy of his notice.

If it had been to his advantage to carry the tale of Violet's misbehaviour to their parents, Arthur would not have hesitated to do so. He thought it more than likely, however, that, instead of praise, he would have received a setdown, not only for tale-bearing, but for having trailed after the duke and her ladyship, who most certainly would have wished to be without his company. Philip, at least, would have wished him elsewhere, he knew, but he told himself that, given the opportunity to choose, Isobel might well have preferred his company to that of the older man.

So it was that the four young ladies, congratulating themselves upon the narrowness of their escape, arose next morning and went out to encourage the viscount and his young friends as they attempted to show off their athletic skills. Emily was so happy to be included as a friend by the other three girls that the fact that she would see nothing of the events did not bother her in the least. It would be no different from all the other exhibitions she had "watched," except that now she was considered one of the group.

Lady Isobel was not present when they went out. Normally a slugabed, she would have arisen if Durban could have been persuaded to take another ride *à deux*, but he had declared that he intended to pit his skills against those of the younger gentlemen, so for the moment she did not think it worth her while to change her custom.

"How wonderful," Violet cried to her friends when they heard that her ladyship would not join them. "If only she could be persuaded to sleep until the house party breaks up, I doubt if anyone would miss her except my cousin."

Arthur would miss her even more than the duke would, she thought but did not say. She had not yet despaired of turning Arthur's interest to her friend Emily. Once he really looked at her, he would forget that near-antidote Isobel.

Since they were in the informality of the country, the gentlemen had doffed their snugly fitted coats to allow them more freedom of movement, something they would never have dared to do in London if ladies were present. Targets had been set up, and several of the gentlemen were eager to display their skill with bows and arrows while others shot at smaller targets with pistols.

Ralph Morely, a youth of about the viscount's age, challenged the others to combat with singlesticks. The sport had lost something of its popularity in late years, but young Ralph had practised it at home and soon showed his skill by soundly defeating James Gillian, to that gentleman's disgust. James had begun to take an interest—which he was careful to keep safely hidden—in Violet, and felt shame at having her see him at a loss, unaware that Violet had spent the entire time in conversation with Sir John and had not noticed who had won or lost.

The victor looked about him for another opponent and saw that the duke had picked up a weapon and was balancing it carelessly in one hand.

"Would you care to try a match with me?" he asked.

Ralph hesitated. Aside from being a person of importance, Durban was almost seven years his senior—almost an old man, in his opinion. It would scarcely be a fair match. Still, the duke looked eager to try, and the young gentleman agreed, thinking he would not give Durban much of a fight.

He was correct in that. It had not occurred to him that Philip was one of the Corinthian set, exercising regularly with his friends at Jackson's Saloon or Cribb's Parlour, or crossing blades with any opponent who would stand up to him. Also, he had often practised with just such an implement as he now held.

In Durban's hands, the stick seemed to have a life of its own, and the self-styled champion several times found himself sitting upon the grass, his head ringing from a sharp blow. At last—it seemed like a long time to him, but was actually only several minutes—he was forced to admit himself beaten.

"It was hardly a fair fight," the duke said, putting out a hand to help him to his feet. "After all, you had just had a stiff match. I doubt if I would have shown to such an advantage if you had been fresh"—an untruth which caused the previously crestfallen Mr. Morely to preen himself anew on his prowess.

"Come along, Stearnes," he cried. "I'll wager that I can best you, even without waiting to rest."

The viscount, who had not shown up well in the shooting matches, had no wish for a bout that he was almost certain to lose—especially when his cousin had just won so handily. Then, too, being knocked about was certain to soil, if not ruin, some of his finery and perhaps even scratch his shining boots. Searching for a feat that would allow him to shine, he said, "No, but I'll match my horse against yours if you like."

"Agreed," cried Mr. Morely, and James Gillian shouted that he also wished to enter the race, for he fancied himself a good horseman and hoped to impress Violet. The trio went off to the stables to have their mounts saddled, arguing amiably about the location and distance of the race. Arthur was determined to have the finish near where the others were standing, as he expected to be the winner and had observed the newest arrival upon the scene.

Roused by the shouts of the combatants and by the equally excited but less noisy encouragement of the ladies, it had belatedly occurred to Lady Isobel that she might be disappointing Durban by not being on hand to watch his exploits. Springing out of bed, she had summoned her dresser—who had been ordered that she was on no account to disturb her mistress before eleven of the clock—and berated her soundly for not being at hand when she was needed. Dressing with a speed unusual to her, she had joined the group in time to see the last of Durban's match with Ralph Morely.

Now she came up and placed her hand upon the duke's arm, saying, "You should not take such chances, Durban. I vow I thought I must swoon at your danger."

Violet's unladylike snort was heard only by the girls standing nearest to her. She knew well how little risk her cousin had run, as did he; and she was certain that Lady Isobel knew it, too.

Laughing, Durban said, "There was no danger at all, my dear. The lad was almost spent. It was hardly fair of me to engage him in the match without giving him a chance to rest. And I have had more practice than he with the stick, I should imagine. The worst I could have suffered would have been a cracked nob."

He twirled the stick about in his hands and looked at Sir John. "What about a bout, Barham?"

The dandy did not shudder as he looked at the stick, but gave the impression that he was about to do so. Like the viscount, he had too much respect for his raiment to risk damaging it in such a match. Also, he did not doubt that Durban would take pleasure in rapping him upon the head as he had done with the boy.

"I thank Your Grace, but no. I have never indulged in the . . . sport. However, if you like, I shall cross foils with you." *That* was a sport fit for gentlemen, his tone implied.

"Agreed," the duke said cheerfully, almost certain that he could win such a bout as well; and even if he could not, it would be worth the exercise. A servant was dispatched to the house for a pair of foils. As they waited, the baronet divested himself of his coat, which was so tight that he required Durban's aid to get out of it.

"Best remove your boots, as well," the duke advised, taking off his own. "The grass is likely to be slippery."

The older man was quite certain that the victory would be his, for he had fought his share of duels. Of course, duels were illegal, but that did not prevent them from taking place from time to time. Even the great Duke of Wellington had broken the law to that extent—not that anything would have been done to *him* if he had been caught. Sir John had never heard of Durban engaging in any duels, but he was said to be a skilled fencer, and it would be a triumph to send him to defeat.

The servants returned, and both gentlemen tested the weight and reach of their weapons before beginning. Soon the clash of steel upon steel was interspersed with the comments between the two as they moved about, each seeking an opening.

Emily had taken several steps away from her friends as the match began, and now it seemed to her from the sounds that the fencers must be coming in her direction. They would be intent upon their bout and unlikely to notice her; fearfully, she took a few steps farther, leaving the lawn for the hard surface of the drive. Interrupting her conversation with the others to turn to look for her newest friend, Violet screamed her name and Emily spun about, facing in the direction she thought the other girl must be.

"Behind you!" Violet shrieked, and at the same time Emily could hear the clatter of approaching hoofbeats. She whirled about, could see the dark shape that was almost upon her, and stepped back, catching her heel upon the edge of the turf and sitting down suddenly while the viscount pulled his galloping mount aside.

It crashed into the one coming up beside it, then stopped in its tracks while the third rider swept ahead to the spot they had chosen to be the finish line, followed by the animal that had been struck. Infuriated at having been beaten another time—and this time in the presence of Lady Isobel—Arthur swung down from the saddle and tugged Emily to her feet, saying angrily, "Why did you not look where you were going, you little fool?"

"I—I am sorry," the girl stammered, still not certain of what had happened, but aware that she had blundered again.

"You should well be," he retorted. "Do you realise that my horse might have been hurt when I had to pull him about like that?"

Everyone had run toward the scene, Violet in the lead. Hearing her brother, she put her arms about Emily and said fiercely, "Do not be such a fool, Arthur. You know it was not Emily who was to blame. Why did it not occur to you to tell us that you were planning to race here?"

The duke had been about to say something, but held his tongue, since Violet had said it for him. The viscount caught his expression as well as that of his sister, and he stood for a moment, fists clenched, wishing he could vent his anger upon the cause of his misfortune. It was exactly like Violet and her stupid friends to do something of this sort and then to put the blame on him instead of where it belonged. He stalked off, leading his horse, and was not appeased when James Gillian caught up with him and said, "Too bad, Stearnes. You would have won that handily if it had not been for the accident."

The viscount turned upon him, cursing him so roundly that Mr. Gillian stopped where he was and let the other go ahead. He was beginning to wonder why he had ever accepted the invitation to Maidencourt. Then his eye fell upon Violet standing with her friends, and a foolish smile spread across his face. How on earth, he wondered, could such a surlyboots as Arthur manage to have so—so *nice* a sister?

=7=

WHILE ARTHUR RETURNED to the stables, muttering imprecations against the girl who had caused him to look foolish before Lady Isobel—who, in truth, had been so interested in the duke's fencing match that she had not noticed what had happened—Emily was assuring her friends that she was not hurt. The horse had not touched her.

"I only turned about too quickly," she explained, "and fell." The other girls, however, had insisted upon helping her to the house. Alerted by Violet's scream, both Durban and Barham had dropped their foils and started forward, only to find themselves pushed aside by the young ladies.

"Please do not say anything about what happened," Emily begged, and her friends reluctantly agreed, unaware that her principal reason for wishing them to remain silent was that she hoped to avoid a scolding from her mama for being clumsy once more. She had not known it was the viscount who had almost ridden her down and who was so angry with her until she heard his voice. If her mama should learn that her daughter had, however inadvertently, done something to overset the viscount, she would be furious and would accuse Emily of trying to ruin her chances. The others who had seen her fall naturally supposed that her friends had reported it, so nothing more was said.

Luncheon was got through with only a few minor mishaps on Emily's part, and these went unnoticed except by the watchful footman, who again wondered that such a quiet-seeming young lady should be so well to live that she could not see her food. However, when her trio of friends suggested a sketching party as an interesting way to spend the afternoon, Emily demurred.

She had learnt to sketch after a fashion, but only when she wore her spectacles; even then, the results were far from admirable. Without them, she knew she would not be able to see the object she was supposed to be sketching, and there was no way that she could pretend to do so. She would have liked to have made one of the group merely for the sake of their company, but she knew that to do so would doubtless bring about a number of questions as to why she did not sketch, and she could not answer without telling them the truth.

"I fear that the sun has given me a touch of migraine," she prevaricated. "But if I can lie down for an hour, I shall recover from it and join you at teatime."

The other girls clustered about her, expressing their sympathy, and Violet asked the question that was on all their minds. "Emily, are you *certain* that you were not hit this morning when you took your tumble? *Did* Arthur's horse strike you after all, and are you only saying that it did not happen so that he will not be blamed for his thoughtlessness?"

"Oh, no," Emily gasped, fearing that, in their concern for her, they might allow the news of the morning's events to reach Lady Harmon's ears. That must not happen. Still, she could perhaps use that as a part of her excuse for not going with them. "No, I was not hurt at all, but . . . but it *was* a bit frightening—although I did not have time to think about it until it was over. I think it might be best for me to rest for a while."

Still only partly reassured as to her well-being, they went off, leaving Emily with a feeling of self-contempt. It was wrong of her to deceive her kind friends, who wished only good for her, but it was far better than to have them pity her for her short-sightedness. Or perhaps they would laugh at her as some sort of a freak. She had again assured them that, with a bit of rest, she would be able to join them at teatime, had waved as long as she could hear their voices, and then had gone to her room.

Despite the morning's events, Emily truly did not feel the need for rest, but having used that as an excuse for returning to her room, she decided that it was time that she looked at the room—really looked at it. The other girls were well on their way to their sketching expedition, and Lady Harmon had accompanied the countess for a drive, pleasantly convinced—and with good reason—that this special attention bespoke a wish on Lady Montayne's part for a closer alliance between the families. There was no chance of anyone coming into the room except Spence, and Spence already knew about the spectacles, so no harm would be done if she saw them.

''If only Mama would permit me to wear them all the time,'' Emily sighed, knowing there was no chance of such a wish coming true. Her mama had ordered that no one should see them until she was safely married.

And what a shock it would be to my husband if I suddenly appeared wearing them, thought Emily. Perhaps to me as well, when I see for the first time what he looks like. He —whoever he may be—might turn out to be very ugly; in that case, it would be better if I could not see him.

She fumbled among the items on the dressing table until she had located her spectacles. As she donned them, the room seemed to spring to life about her, as always happened. She already knew that the bed was set high above the floor, having fallen both yesterday and this morning in getting out of it, and she had drawn the hangings close enough to her eyes to learn that the satin was a soft colour between blue and green.

Now she could see for the first time the tiny gold cherubs that pinned back the hangings and matched others frolicking up the sides of the huge mirror above the dressing table.

Each of those around the mirror held a musical instrument; one played a harp, another a lute, and a third blew upon a horn which was so long that still another had to help to hold it aloft. Others had instruments whose names Emily did not know.

Laughing at the comical expression on the tiny faces, especially on that of the fat-cheeked one who seemed to be struggling to produce a note on his long horn, she moved on to examine the delicate carving upon the bedposts. She had already traced it with her fingers, but now she became aware that it was matched by those upon the dressing table and the secretaire that stood in the corner. She also found that the colour of the bed hangings was repeated in the drapes and in the intricate pattern of the elegant carpet.

It was truly a beautiful room, and she could have spent much longer looking about her, but there might be a chance to see more of it at another time. Just now, if she hurried, perhaps she would be able to see something of the rest of the house. Catching up her workbag, so that if anyone was around she could pretend that she had brought it downstairs to work, she carefully opened the door. No one was in the hall, so she kept her spectacles in place as she went out, admiring the ornamental sconces and the delicate gold scrollwork upon the bedroom doors.

A number of pictures hung between the doors, and she went from one to another, looking at them with pleasure. She could not identify the artists, having had no opportunity to study such a subject, but she enjoyed the combinations of colours upon the canvases. Some colours were muted, others almost violent, she thought, but all were pleasing to the eye.

Hearing the sound of footsteps coming along the hall from the servants' wing, she hurried to the front staircase and made her way down it, admiring the carving upon the stairposts, but pausing at the landing to make certain that no one was below. She smiled as she recognised the suit of Sir Edmund's armour, which she had greeted on the day of her arrival, and made another curtsy to it as she passed.

At the foot of the stairs, she stood for some time, gazing about the Great Hall with its fireplace, which was large enough that a man might stand upright within it; the high, rough-beamed ceiling; and the windows near the ceiling —taken from the demolished abbey—whose colours made rainbows upon the black and white chequered marble of the floor.

She had been told that afternoon tea would be served in the Gold Saloon, and this would be a good opportunity for her to see it. The gentlemen appeared to be out following some interests of their own, and the mothers of the other girls were doubtless resting. She opened the door a crack and made certain that the room was empty, then slipped within and closed the door quickly behind her.

Placing her workbag upon a chair, she wandered about the room, noting that the furniture down here was even more elaborately carved than that in her bedroom. The back of one sofa bore a stain that the servants had not been able to eradicate, and Emily flushed at sight of it, knowing this must be where she had flung the tea when she tripped. Quickly, she went on to the cabinets that were scattered about the large room. All were filled with miniatures, jewelled snuff-boxes, or delicate figurines, and she stood before each of them for some time, marvelling at the beauty of the objects.

Glancing upward, she saw that the ceiling was painted, and gazed until her neck ached at the nymphs and satyrs that frolicked about a central group of gods and goddesses —either Greek or Roman, she supposed from having seen similar pictures in books. She blushed at the antics and the state of undress of some of the figures and wondered that a noble family would display such works to their friends.

Perhaps the painting was done so long ago that no one pays any attention to it, she mused. Or it may be that any number of houses have such work but that I have not seen it.

She wondered if she dared risk going outside the house to take a look at it, but decided that must wait for another day. She had been alone for quite a time, and some of the others might be returning soon; she must not be caught wearing her spectacles. Still, she might at least have a quick look from one of the windows that opened upon the lawn.

Crossing the room toward the windows, she caught sight of three slim volumes lying upon a table, their leather covers lettered in gold. Curious, she turned the top one about to read the title: *Glenarvon*.

During her season in London, she had heard a great deal about Lady Caroline Lamb's literary effort, but Lady Harmon had refused to allow her to procure a copy, saying that she would be far too occupied while they were in the city to have any time for reading. The truth was that many of the comments which her ladyship had heard about the book convinced her that it was not suitable for a young female to read. She did not approve of her daughter's interest in books, fearing that it might interfere with her chances of snaring a husband, and it was only Lord Harmon's insistence that she be permitted to read which had prevented his wife from forbidding Emily ever to open a book.

Of course, Mama never wants me to read anything, thought Emily, and I think that she only used the rumours she heard about *Glenarvon* as an excuse to keep me from reading it.

She picked up the first volume, thinking that if it proved to be interesting enough to take to her room, she might read it after the party had broken up for the night. Many of the remarks that had been made about the book caused her to wonder about it, but she would not condemn it unread, as her mama had done. Lady Caroline was supposed to have written the novel to revenge herself upon Lord Byron for breaking off his *affaire* with her and had cast him as the villainous hero of the story. Of course, both her ladyship and the poet were married, and not to each other—still, during her short stay in London, Emily had learnt that such a situation was not in the least unusual. Many married ladies had liaisons, but most of them were more discreet about them.

The aspect of *Glenarvon* which intrigued readers was that Lady Caro had not only used Byron in the book, and had used him infamously, but that many of the characters were also supposed to be thinly disguised descriptions of the author's husband, family, and friends. Some people in London were said to have devised a key to the book, but Emily had never seen it.

During her stay in London, she had met several of those who were said to be in the story. Not Lady Caro's aunt, Georgina, Duchess of Devonshire, of course, as she had died some time before—which had not prevented the graceless authoress from including her in the book and chronicling many of her real, or imagined, indiscretions. Emily had not met Lord Byron, either, for Lady Harmon had felt that the rumours about his private life—whether true or not—made him an undesirable person to be introduced to a young female. He had been at some of the parties Emily had attended; she had not seen him, but had heard that he customarily stood about trying to look like one of his own heroes.

Having read for many years before being fitted for her spectacles, Emily was in the habit of reading without them. She slipped them into her workbag for safekeeping; if she laid them down somewhere, she would not be able to find them. She opened the book and brought it close to her eyes, determined only to glance at it now to learn whether it would be worth taking to her room. She read a paragraph, then another, and was lost.

"*Could* people really behave as outrageously as this?" she murmured. And even if they did so, how could Lady Caroline write in such a fashion about people she knew? And did she truly see herself as the unfortunate heroine of the story?

A sharp box upon her ear brought Emily back to reality, and she looked up in dismay at her mama, hoping that her words had not been overheard. At least, she supposed that the bulk towering over her was Lady Harmon; it was unlikely that anyone else would chastise her. Her ladyship's angry voice confirmed the suspicion.

"Have you not better sense than to be sitting here where someone might see you *reading*? It is fortunate that I was the first to come in. Have I not told you any number of times that nothing will put a gentleman off so quickly as the thought that a young lady is *bookish*? And why are you wasting your time in here instead of being out somewhere where Lord Stearnes can see you?"

"The gentlemen had all gone somewhere together." At least, she thought they had all gone, and had not heard any of them returning.

"Then with his sister? I have been doing everything I can to impress the countess with the idea that you would be the perfect daughter-in-law, and you do nothing to help. You could very well be encouraging her to speak to her brother on your behalf."

"Violet and her other friends are sketching. You know that I cannot sketch."

"If only you would make the effort, you might do so. But this is all a part of the way your father has allowed you to behave, sitting about with your nose between the pages of a book instead of doing something useful. How you ever expect to attract a husband, I do not know. If you must stay in here instead of being with the others, you might at least take out your needlework and be stitching upon it when everyone comes in. Such industry is always appealing."

Emily sighed and caught the workbag which Lady Harmon had snatched up and tossed into her lap. She was thankful that her spectacles had not fallen out of the bag—she could feel them through the cloth—for the fact that she had brought them downstairs would be cause for another scolding. It was fortunate, too, that her mama had not been interested enough to ask her what book it was she found so fascinating. It could be that Lady Harmon would not have remembered the gossip about *Glenarvon*; she had never cared what might lie between the pages of a book, not even having been given to a taste for novel reading in her own green years.

Obediently, Emily tucked the book out of sight beneath the edge of her skirt, hoping that she might still be able to get it to her room unseen, for she had enjoyed the little she had read and would like to finish it before her stay at Maidencourt was over.

Taking the piece of needlework out of her bag, she selected a length of brilliant blue silk. If she must do needlework, a task she had never particularly enjoyed, she preferred to work in bright colours whenever possible.

Locating her needle by feeling about her embroidery until she had pricked her finger, she brought needle and silk close to her eyes and managed, after several vain attempts, to get the thread through the tiny eye of the needle. As she spread out her work, the needle slipped from her grasp, and only by catching quickly at the bright floss was she able to keep it from falling to the carpet, where she would not have been able to find it without getting down upon her knees and groping about for it—an act that would have infuriated Lady Harmon. Holding the needle firmly, she bent low over her work, trying to see where she had made her last stitches.

"For heaven's sake, Emily, do not crouch over your work as if something ailed you," Lady Harmon said crossly, seating herself upon a sofa and smoothing the skirts of her mauve brocade about her ample person. She had been careful to avoid the tea-stained sofa, for who knew whether the tea might not mar her gown? Also, it was an unpleasant reminder of Emily's latest blunder. She was surprised that the servants had not removed the sofa until it could be recovered. "You have been taught better than that. Sit up and go about your work in a ladylike manner."

Emily straightened, repressing an impulse to bring the work up to her eyes so that she could see what she was doing; she was certain that her ladyship would object to that as well. Instead she sat thrusting her needle haphazardly into the cloth, pricking her finger several more times in the process. She hoped that the injured spots were not bleeding upon her work; with all the labour she had already put into the piece, it would be dreadful to have to throw it away and start anew. As it was, she knew that every stitch she was doing now would probably have to be ripped out and done over when she was alone.

Even that, however, was better than attempting to argue upon the subject with her mama, who, despite her own excellent eyesight, was never able to see that her daughter was having problems. To her ladyship, the appearance Emily presented to others was of prime importance, for others —and especially gentlemen—were prone to judge only by appearance.

Lady Harmon smiled now as she watched Emily, sitting up as she should and working industriously. If only the viscount might come in soon and see what a charming picture she made as she plied her needle. Taking out a bit of work of her own, Lady Harmon decided that if Lord Stearnes *should* come in before the others, she would make some excuse to leave the two of them alone. It was not proper, of course, but in the circumstances. . . .

Heaven grant, she said silently, that Emily will have the wit to know what to do in such a case.

To her disappointment, the viscount did not appear. Instead, it was the sketching party that returned first, the two visiting ladies full of enthusiasm about the wonderful opportunities for their artistic endeavours. Violet was happy to have pleased them, but enquired anxiously about Emily's migraine, causing Lady Harmon to look suspiciously at her daughter while Emily stammered that it was completely gone. They were accompanied by an obese, middle-aged, foppishly dress gentleman whom Violet introduced as Sir Hayden Monke.

"A neighbour," she explained. "Sir Hayden's acres lie just beyond our own. He was riding by just as we finished sketching, and we have invited him to accompany us back here for tea."

Her ladyship was being more polite than truthful. Sir Hayden had seen the young ladies at their sketching and—as Violet privately suspected—had lingered out of sight until they were nearly ready to leave, then had appeared and had insisted upon giving them his escort, aware that Violet could scarcely avoid inviting him to remain for tea.

He had every intention of managing to have himself invited for dinner as well. Having a prodigious appetite, he much preferred taking his meals at the expense of others and was aware of the lavish table set by the Leslies, as well as the skill of their French chef. Also, it was possible that the earl and countess would have guests who were worthy of his attention.

A brief examination of the room showed him that his hopes in this respect were fulfilled. Like the Prince Regent, whom he copied to the best of his ability, Sir Hayden had a preference for ladies who were past their first youth. He frankly ogled Lady Harmon, admiring her size, which nearly matched his own.

Lady Harmon, however, had no liking for fops of any age, and had a special aversion to older ones whose corsets creaked when they moved. As she had always refused to see herself as she really was, she could not understand how anyone could allow himself to become so grossly overweight. The idea that such a person—from his actions, she would scarcely call him a gentleman—might think that he would appeal to her was revolting.

She met Sir Hayden's flirtatious glances with so disdainful a look that he thought it prudent to withdraw from her vicinity and wait until some of the other members of the party arrived. No doubt there would be some other lady who would appreciate him properly. Surely those childish friends of Lady Violet must have relatives who were . . . more mature.

In an effort to demonstrate to the haughty dowager—for so he termed her—that he had not been at all impressed by her withering glances, he strolled idly about the room, picking up several items from the different cabinets, examining and replacing them. Some of them might have gone into his pockets if he could have been certain that he was unobserved. He was certain, however, that under their chatter the young ladies—and doubtless the older one as well, despite her show of indifference—were casting admiring glances in his direction, and he did not wish to be seen doing anything that would make future visits to Maidencourt impossible.

Coming at last to the chair where Emily—who had at last convinced Violet and her friends that her migraine had truly disappeared, just as she had said it would—still thrust her needle in and out of her work, he leaned over her shoulder. A portion of the pattern, he noted, had been well done, but what the young lady was doing now was deplorable. Those ragged stitches. . . . Obviously a governess or some other person had done the first part of the work, and the young lady was only pretending to be a needlewoman.

In a manner, he could sympathise with her wish to be thought something she was not. However, he fancied himself a connoisseur of all the arts, and was frequently consulted by ladies of his acquaintance who knew no better than to be flattered by his opinion. It was clear to him that this one was in need of advice, and he was prepared to give it.

"Should that blue not be down there?" he asked, pointing to a spot upon the lower part of the work, then yelping as Emily drove her needle into his unseen hand.

=8=

EMILY WAS IN disgrace once more. Lady Harmon had strongly disapproved of everything about Sir Hayden, from his attire —which would have been better suited to someone twenty years younger and several stone lighter than he—to his ponderous gallantries. Nonetheless, he was a guest, and it was unforgivable of Emily to have stabbed him with her needle. After all, he had only been attempting to point out the mistakes she had been making in her embroidery.

What was far worse was the fact that the girl, given a hint as to what she must have done when the gentleman cried out in pain, had leapt to her feet. The action had sent the hidden volume to the floor, where Laura Maugham had pounced upon it.

"*Glenarvon!*" she cried happily. "Oh, I have heard that it is delightfully scandalous, and I have been wishing to read it, but Mama would not permit me to do so. Tell me, Emily, is it truly as naughty as I have been told?"

Emily heard Lady Harmon's angry gasp as it was revealed that her daughter had not only been reading, but had been reading a forbidden book. Dismayed, the girl turned and fled in what she hoped was the direction of the doorway, running full tilt into a figure that had just entered the room. A strong arm went about her, steadying her, and a deep voice, tinged with amusement, asked, "In trouble again, are you, little one?"

As Emily stammered an apology and attempted to pass

him, Lady Harmon came up behind her and caught her arm in a painful grip, saying, "I must again beg pardon for my child's clumsiness, Your Grace."

Hardly waiting for the duke's polite disavowal, she propelled the girl out of the room, which was already buzzing with the tale of Emily's latest escapade, and half-dragged her up the stairs to her bedroom, where she proceeded to scold her roundly for her behaviour.

"It is bad enough to let it be known—and after I had warned you not to do so—that you had been reading," she chided, going first to the subject which seemed to her the most reprehensible, "but to have everyone know that you had been reading such a book. . . ."

In truth, she knew little about the book, except for some hints given by friends, some of whom had read it and others who had only imagined what must lie beneath its covers. According to them—especially those who had *not* read it—it was truly scandalous. And to have it be known that her daughter was given to a liking for such a book!

"Everyone will be saying that you must be fast, to have such tastes, and what the countess will say when she finds out what you have been reading!" She ignored the fact that, since Emily must have found the book here, it would have to belong to the countess; besides, Lady Montayne was a mature woman, and married. What she might choose to read need not be proper for a young girl.

"And then, to treat one of the countess's guests in such a fashion when he was only trying to be kind to you—and not to mention nearly knocking the *duke* off his feet. I am deeply ashamed of you, Emily, and I think it might be best if you did not come down to tea. Perhaps by dinnertime, I can persuade them to forgive you."

She went out, and Emily huddled upon her bed, happy to be free from the necessity of taking tea with those downstairs who had witnessed her many errors, and wishing that she might remain in her room for the rest of the visit. It seemed to her that every time she left its shelter she got into fresh trouble.

It would have been best if Violet had not asked her parents to invite us here, she said to herself, feeling across the bedcovers for the workbag and the offending piece of embroidery that her mama had flung down beside her. Then Mama would not have got the idea that I could make Lord Stearnes propose to me. Even if he wished to do so, which I am certain he does not, the countess would forbid it.

She drew her spectacles from the bag and started to don them, then hid them quickly as she heard her door open. Mama was angry enough with her now, she thought, without someone seeing her in spectacles. It was Violet who slipped into the room, giggling as she flung herself down beside Emily and put both arms about her.

"Oh, that was the most wonderful thing for you to have done," she cried. "I wish that *I* had thought of doing it long ago. But then I never would have had the needle, for my embroidery was always so poor that my governess gave up trying to teach me. Of course, I *might* have stabbed him with the garden shears; I am certain Papa would have been willing to provide them. Or something. . . . Anyway, Sir Hayden has decided not to stay for tea after all. Someone told him that you had spilt tea on Isobel the other evening, and I think he might have feared you would do the same to him."

"No, no, I would not. That was an accident. Of course, my stabbing the gentleman was an accident, also; I did not realise that he had put his hand in my way. Besides, Mama has told me that I ought not to come down to tea. I ought not to have come here at all; I am forever doing something clumsy. Your guests—"

"Oh, Sir Hayden is not a guest—not really. The man is so encroaching. He *insisted* upon accompanying us back to the house, saying that we ought not to be out alone—and on our own grounds. Nothing I could say would dissuade him. It never does. And he positively *toadeats* Mama and Papa. I am

VALPARAISO-PORTER COUNTY
PUBLIC LIBRARY
VALPARAISO, INDIANA 46383

certain that they must be as happy as I that you drove him away—although I suppose they would think it impolite to say so.''

She paused for breath, then giggled again. ''As for Isobel, she is nothing more than a spiteful old cat. I wish that you had poured an entire pot of tea on her—boiling, too. Not content with trying to get her claws into my cousin, who is old enough that he ought to be able to see that she is merely after his title, she has been trying to attach Arthur as well. That was why—'' She broke off and clapped her hands over her mouth.

''That was why . . . ?'' Emily prompted.

''Do not be angry with me, dear Emily. I have never tried matchmaking before, and I hope you will not dislike it. I only thought that if Arthur could but see you, he might forget Isobel and form a *tendre* for you. But it is not only to get him away from her, believe me. You are so beautiful —and sweet. I would love to have you for a sister.''

Emily stared at the other girl's face, now near enough to her own that she could see it clearly. How could anyone think *she* was beautiful, compared to Violet with her dusky curls and creamy complexion? Still, the viscount was her brother and might discount her looks for that reason. Brothers seemed not to think highly of their sisters; she knew that George frequently referred to her as a ''scarecrow,'' but she had always feared that he was right.

Since the viscount was as dark as his sister, it might be that he would prefer someone who was fairer. Could she— possibly—take his attention away from Lady Isobel? Emily had not been able to see her ladyship closely, but thought she must be beautiful indeed.

''Mama likes you, too, I know that she does,'' Violet was saying, ''and Papa has said that you are a taking little thing and that you remind him of one of his roses. Believe me, he cannot offer higher praise than that to anyone.''

Colour flooded Emily's face. It would seem that she had

the approval of the entire family, save for the viscount. If he had even the slightest interest in her, he was concealing it well. Too well, in fact. Perhaps, too, there was one other member of the family who had a reason for disliking her.

"The duke—"

"Oh, he does not matter one way or the other, except that I suppose he would be grateful to you if you could attract Arthur, so that he would not continue trailing after Isobel like a lost puppy. I do not see how my own brother can be such a ninnyhammer; everyone else is quite sensible. But if Arthur does turn his interest to you—"

"But the duke—" Emily still remembered her mama's angry words on the subject. "I spilt the tea on Lady Isobel, and I ran into him downstairs just now."

"Oh, phoo. He will not care for your running into him; he is large enough to take care of himself. And as for the other, he told Isobel that she was too hard on you when it had been an accident." Violet dismissed her cousin in favour of a topic much more interesting to her.

"I have been reading *Glenarvon*, too—in secret; I do not think Mama would approve of my doing so. Of course, she has not forbidden me to read it or I would not, and I know that she has read it herself, for she and her friends talk about it, although they stop when they know I am near. Tell me, do you think Caro Lamb actually pictures *herself* as the unfortunate heroine?"

"I have heard that some people think so, and I have wondered—but I have not read enough, of course, to be able to have an opinion about it," Emily confessed, and Violet offered to smuggle all three volumes to her so that she might finish the story before she went home.

She stayed gossiping with Emily about their season in London and about the guests of the house party. Sir John's name came frequently into the conversation, possibly more frequently than the young lady herself was aware. At last, Spence came in to inform her, with the sternness allowed to an old and loved servant, that teatime was long past and that her ladyship's abigail was waiting to dress her for dinner.

Reassured by Violet's confidence that the family looked upon her with approval, Emily found that her reluctance to join the party below had vanished. Gowned by Spence in a white muslin sprigged with forget-me-nots, bound with a sash of the same shade of blue and with a matching riband in her curls, she was again assigned to Arthur as a partner and, despite his continued neglect, contrived at least to get through the meal without incident.

In the drawing room after dinner, Violet, Laura, and Marjorie clustered about her, telling her that she should have been with them on their sketching expedition, and poking fun at Sir Hayden's attempts to get an invitation to tea. With her friends inserting their comments and occasionally contradicting—for each of them preferred her own version of what had happened—Violet repeated the story she had told upstairs.

Sir Hayden had arrived at the exact moment that the trio began to gather up their sketching materials. Being strangers, the others had considered this only a coincidence, but to Violet, who knew him, the opportuneness of his coming was suspicious. Her friends began to share her suspicion when the gentleman insisted again and again that he would not permit them to make the journey back to the house without his protection.

"I reminded him—indeed, I think I became almost rude about it—that we were still upon the grounds of Maidencourt and that we were therefore in no need of protection. When he spoke of the possibility of poachers, I was near to telling him that the only intruder was himself."

"But nothing that Violet said made the slightest difference to him. I vow, the man has the hide of . . . of. . . ."

"A crocodile," Laura supplied, and Marjorie smiled her thanks.

"Indeed he has, and he would not leave us."

"He knew that if he came with us, Mama would have no choice but to ask him to stay for tea," Violet explained again.

"But you routed him, Emily—thoroughly; you are a true heroine."

Under the praise from her friends, Emily began to think that she had done nothing so terrible, after all, despite what Lady Harmon had said. The countess, of course, said nothing to her guests about what had happened, being too well bred to voice her opinion of her neighbour. Privately, however, she and her husband laughed about the incident.

"I fear Miss Harmon's treatment was a bit drastic," she said, "but I can understand how she must have been driven to it, for I imagine that Sir Hayden was his usual self."

"Never did care for that man-milliner," was the earl's comment. "The gel did the right thing to get rid of him for us. Got a head on her shoulders—and a pretty one, at that."

"What would you think of her as a daughter-in-law?"

He turned to look at her for a moment, then shook his head. "Don't think Arthur has enough sense to offer for her. Pity; she would be good for him."

Lady Montayne agreed wholeheartedly. Despite her growing fondness for Emily, however, she had the memory of the other evening's catastrophe in mind and thought it best not to ask Emily to hand around the tea again.

Instead, she requested Laura to do so, a task that somewhat alleviated the young lady's feeling of being mistreated. Whenever the gentlemen joined the ladies after dinner, she would lament anew that her papa's hardheartedness in refusing to permit her to bring her harp had been responsible for her inability to entertain them—unaware that most of the members of the house party silently agreed with her parent's outspoken comment that they were fortunate to be spared her performance.

Emily was all too happy to be relieved of the duty of serving, for she, too, feared a repetition of the earlier accident. Perhaps the only one who was not pleased at the new arrangement was Lady Harmon, who had viewed the countess's pairing Emily with her daughter for the service as a sign that the family approved of the girl.

Even Lady Harmon, however, was forced to admit—only to herself, of course—that there was always the element of risk in having Emily perform such tasks. The child was unquestionably prone to accidents and did not shine at such times.

After the young ladies had finished serving the tea, a certain gentleman—to Emily, no more than a blur of vivid colour—approached the group. It seemed to her that this was the same figure who had sat beside her at dinner; perhaps the viscount was deigning to notice her after all.

She flashed him a welcoming smile, then shrank back in her chair, aware that she had again made one of her errors when Violet said, in a voice which betrayed her feelings, "John, I really should give you a severe scold. I was afraid —that is, I thought—that you were intending to desert me for the evening, and I should not like that."

"My dear Lady Violet, certainly no one would ever wish to desert you," the baronet said in such caressing tones that the young lady flushed with pleasure and Emily once more told herself that she must have imagined the warmth with which he had kissed her hand the first evening.

Sir John stayed, talking with them for some time, every remark laden with compliments for Violet. That young woman was far too besotted to be aware of the glances he frequently cast in the direction of Emily, who was too near-sighted to see them. At length, the gentleman decided, reluctantly, that he must have been wrong in his earlier estimation of this young lady. Was she a tease, blowing hot and then cold? Or, he preened himself on the thought, *was* she interested in him but merely too clever to cast out lures when Violet was about? Ah well, there would be other occasions before the party ended.

Emily would have been deeply shocked had she realised the motives that Sir John was attributing to her. It was clear, even to her, that Violet had a *tendre* for the baronet and, although she could judge only by his voice, she believed him to return that regard. Doubtless he would be offering for her friend quite soon.

Both young ladies were mistaken in their estimate of Sir John. Although he had long ago faced the fact that it might become necessary for him to seek a rich wife, he did not propose to do so as long as he could avoid it.

He enjoyed his rakish bachelorhood, just as he enjoyed being the idol of a number of young men of the stamp of Lord Stearnes, who aped his fashions and attempted to ape his life-style. When Stearnes had rather diffidently suggested that he become a member of the house party, Sir John had pretended to give the matter some thought before saying languidly, "Good of you to ask me, my boy. If I can arrange my schedule to make room for the visit, I shall come—for a day or two."

The truth was that he was never completely out of Dun Territory, and at present moment his creditors were becoming much too demanding to please him. The invitation could not have come at a more opportune time and, while he realised that his stay in the country would only defer the moment of reckoning, there was always the chance that something might turn up to save him.

He had been vaguely aware that Lord Stearnes had a sister, but she was half his age, and he had paid no attention to her in London, which was filled with more exciting game. Now he had become certain that she and her considerable dowry might be his for the asking.

If the earl and the countess had not heard too much about his exploits, and if he could prevent that young idiot Stearnes from boasting about the very things which would be best kept secret, he might offer for Lady Violet. Fortunate for him that Stearnes's mind was presently set upon his pursuit of Lady Isobel and he had not had time to fling the cat among the pigeons. An alliance with the Leslies would certainly work to Sir John's advantage. To be son-in-law to an earl and cousin to a duke would be no light matter and should serve to discourage those creditors who were becoming importunate.

Still, he said to himself, just because I *might* become riveted, that need not interefere with my enjoyment. And if a pretty little filly casts out lures in my direction, as that one has been doing, I certainly see no reason why I should discourage her. I deserve a bit of a change from Violet's clinging ways. Of course, since she and Violet are such close friends, the girl will have to be careful. She is wise not to show too much interest when others are about.

After exchanging several more remarks with Violet, his so ardent in both word and tone as to have her blushing and stammering with pleasure, he strolled away toward the far side of the room, where several gentlemen were standing. When he was certain that her ladyship could no longer see him, he turned and leered at Emily, priding himself on an easy conquest when he saw her smile—unaware that Emily had lost sight of him before he had taken more than a dozen steps from them and that she was smiling at something Violet was murmuring to her.

With the removal of the tea tray, the members of the party began to move toward their bedrooms. In passing, Lady Harmon gave her daughter a pleasant, and unseen, smile, happy that Emily had done nothing wrong this evening. It would have been better if she had been in the viscount's company, but he had been with his friends for most of the evening, and even she could not wish Emily to approach a group of gentlemen. It would be most improper. At least Emily had been with his sister, so it had not been a bad evening after all from her mama's point of view.

Upon returning to her room, Emily discovered that Violet had somehow found time to smuggle all three volumes of *Glenarvon* upstairs for her. After Spence had extinguished the candles and left her, she relit the one beside the bed and spent an hour revelling in the strange and twisted world created by Lady Caroline Lamb.

When sleep threatened, she crept from her bed—misjudging its height as usual and tumbling to the floor—and hid the books beneath the garments in one of her drawers. She was certain that Spence would not betray her —after all, she must already have seen the books—but it was best that they should be out of sight in case her mama should come into the room.

Putting out the light once more, she fell asleep, wondering at the feeling that could cause a young lady of Quality to disguise herself as a page to follow her lover about; did such things happen only in books? No, she recalled that Lady Caroline had actually done such a thing in pursuit of Lord Byron. Was it possible that *she* would ever have such a strong feeling about . . . about Arthur? It was most likely that it did not happen to many people.

After enjoying the morning chocolate and bread and butter that Spence brought her, Emily descended the stairs, merely touching Sir Edmund's suit of armour with one forefinger as she passed, for someone might be watching and she did not wish to be thought foolish, as she would if she were seen curtsying to it once more. Following the sound of voices, she found that the other young people were in the breakfast room.

The young ladies had fortified themselves as Emily had done, in the privacy of their rooms. Now they were sitting over cups of cooling tea and toying with their food to give the impression that they were dainty eaters—an act which fooled no one. Violet and her friends hailed Emily, and she carefully made her way in their direction, circling around the vivid green figure that must be Lady Isobel.

She could not see how her ladyship shrank away as she passed, but she did hear the male voice that said reprovingly, "Isobel, you are behaving childishly," and the mutter from across the table, "Not at all; the girl's a menace."

Emily did not doubt that she was the menace to whom he was referring, but she did not know the owner of the voice or his reason for the comment. The only thing she had done —recently—was to run her needle into Sir Hayden's hand, and it seemed that only her mama had seen anything so very wrong in that.

She groped for a chair, found it was being held for her, and slipped into it with a murmur of thanks. The three young girls began to talk at once, telling of their plans for the morning.

"It is not to be a real hunt, of course, for this is not the season for hunting. But that is not going to stop us; we are going on a mock hunt. One of the grooms has been sent out to lay a paper trail for us, and we shall follow just as if we were after a fox. It promises to be most exciting."

"It was Isobel's idea," Violet said bitterly, but in a voice so low that it could not be heard by the lady at the other end of the table. "I am certain she only thought of it to show everyone how well she looks on her horse."

The other two, since neither of them had any reason for disliking everything to do with Lady Isobel, were more enthusiastic.

"Hurry and get into your habit," Laura said. "We plan to leave in half an hour."

"I cannot," Emily protested. "I . . . I do not ride."

Her father had made an attempt to make a horsewoman out of her, but had come to the conclusion that his efforts were wasted when it was proven that she would never be able to manage her pony without a leading string. He had not known then that the trouble was that she could not see as far as her horse's ears, so she had no way of guiding it.

She might have been able to manage more easily now that she had her spectacles, but Lord Harmon had long given over any idea of teaching her. In any case, she would not have been able to wear her spectacles today.

"But you must come." She recognised the voice as Lady Isobel's. "I absolutely insist upon it, Miss Harmon. Everyone will be going, and I cannot allow your absence to spoil our 'hunt.' "

Emily was surprised at the pleasant tone and at her ladyship's insistence upon Emily's joining the group. She had thought that Lady Isobel still disliked her for having spilt the tea on her gown.

In that, she was correct. Lady Isobel had *not* forgiven her for spoiling an expensive gown, and she resented the fact that both the duke and his aunt thought she should forget the matter. It was Durban's championship of the chit she found most galling. He had twice taken her to task about the matter—and before others.

If the girl was telling the truth when she said she could not ride, she was certain to make a poor showing, possibly getting in the way of the others and in general proving that she, Isobel, had done right to avoid her. Like any other gentleman, Durban was mad for sports and would doubtless be given a disgust of the girl if she made a fool of herself. On the other hand, he would remember that her ladyship had respected his wishes and had made an effort to be kind to the troublesome girl.

"I do not . . . I have no habit."

Emily was resolved that *nothing* could persuade her to join the group. It was foolish beyond anything to think of trying to ride when she would not be able to see which way the others were going. If only she had pleaded another migraine, she might have been able to remain safely in her room this morning.

"That is no problem," Marjorie assured her. "I brought two habits with me, not being able to decide which I might wish to wear. We are almost of a size, and you may borrow the green one."

It was not so vivid a hue as Lady Isobel's, and Marjorie was certain that her pale prettiness would be completely eclipsed by her ladyship's magnificence. She would show up to better advantage in the celestial blue; and since she would be doing Emily a favour by lending her the habit, the pomona green would do very well for that.

Emily was trying to find words to decline the offer without giving her true reason for not wishing to ride, when Lady Harmon came into the room. Hearing the plans the young people had been making and of Marjorie's offer, she looked about the room and saw that the viscount was already in a fashionably cut riding coat, buckskins, and white-topped boots. Emily *must not* be left behind this time.

"Of course you must go with the others," she said. "You will spoil their sport if you do not go, and you would not wish to do that. It is most kind of Miss Allenby to lend you a habit, since you did not bring your own."

She had not been in the room when Emily had declared that she had no habit, but no one thought this contradictory, being certain that the girl had merely meant that she had not brought one with her. Some might have thought that fact odd, for it was the custom to ride at country parties.

Lady Harmon had not liked to ride when she was young, and for a number of years could not have done so if she wished, unless her husband had brought a draft horse to carry her. She did not realise, therefore, exactly how dangerous it might be for her daughter to attempt to ride blindly in a fast-moving group such as this would be. She thought only that this would be an excellent opportunity to throw Emily and the viscount together and added coyly, "I am certain that Lord Stearnes will look after you. Will you not, my lord?"

Arthur had no idea why Isobel wished to include such a

tiresome brat in what had promised to be an interesting ride. Since she did wish it, however, he would do nothing to throw a rub in her way.

"You may rest easy on that point, Lady Harmon," he said. "I shall see that she is well mounted."

He did not add that as soon as he had seen Emily into her saddle, he planned to be as far away from her—and as close to Isobel—as was possible.

"There, I knew you would do so, and the matter is settled," Lady Harmon said cheerfully. Lord Stearnes would look after Emily, and if she should prove a slight bit awkward in mounting and dismounting, it was a wonderful opportunity to fall into the gentleman's arms. "Now, run along, Emily, and get into the habit that Miss Allenby has been kind enough to offer you. It will not do to keep the others waiting."

=9=

EMILY WAS APPALLED that her mama should think for a moment that she would be able to ride. Why could she not understand how impossible it was for her to do anything of the kind? But then, Mama never did understand how her near-sightedness prevented her from doing many things that others did.

For an instant, she was near to blurting out the truth, but realised in time that she would never be forgiven if she allowed these people to think her an object of pity—or fun. Still, short of falling upon the stairs and claiming to have sprained her ankle, she did not see how she could escape.

Hearing Lady Harmon's instructions to her daughter, Lady Isobel said, with the laugh which one admirer—not Durban, alas—had told her was like tinkling bells, "I have no doubt that you think we are being silly to play such a childish game —for indeed, we cannot have a true hunt at this season— but a paper chase will give us some exercise. I thought it would be a pleasant way to spend a morning; and you know how the gentlemen enjoy their sport."

She moved a step closer to the duke as she spoke, smiling up at him as if to say that the entire affair was being planned for his benefit. To Lady Harmon, however, the word "gentleman" meant the viscount, and she congratulated herself upon having paired him with Emily so easily. She thought of the ride merely as a pleasant outing with none of the hazards of a true hunt. By the time the party returned, who knew but what her daughter might be well on her way to becoming Lady Stearnes?

There might be any number of opportunities—or so she had heard—for intimacy on such an occasion. A gentleman might clasp a lady's waist to lift her into or out of the saddle. If the viscount did so and Emily had the wit to melt into his arms, he might easily be persuaded to make an avowal—or at least to commit himself to the point where an avowal must soon be forthcoming. Seeing only her daughter's triumph, she beamed upon the assemblage and said, "Do hurry, Emily, and change. You are being impolite to make everyone wait upon you."

She left them and went off to admire some of the wonders of the house and imagine how it would be when Emily was mistress here. Of course, that would not be for some time; the young people would have their own home, and doubtless it would be an elegant one, but one day Lord Stearnes would be Earl of Montayne. And Emily *must* be his countess.

As Emily went up the stairs with her arm linked in Marjorie's—she was beginning to be able to tell the two fair-haired girls apart by their voices—she was wondering if it would be possible for her to allow the others to ride ahead of her, then put on her spectacles and follow them. She thought she could manage to stay on the horse's back, since this was not really to be a hunt. It was the problem of seeing where she was going that troubled her.

Marjorie, however, caught up the riding dress and went along to Emily's room, chattering to her while Spence was helping her into the green habit. Emily had no opportunity of getting the spectacles out of her reticule without the other girl's curiosity being aroused, and she was certain by now that Marjorie would wish to know all about the spectacles and would be only too eager to tell about them. It would be worse than useless to ask her to keep the secret; within moments, everyone in the house party would know that Emily Harmon wore spectacles.

Lady Harmon would never forgive her if that happened. Emily was accustomed to her mama's anger about something or other, but if word of her spectacles got out, she did not doubt that they would be taken away from her and that Lady Harmon would never permit her to wear them again.

Feeling more miserable with every moment that passed, Emily started for the door, was stopped by Spence to have the long skirt of the habit draped over her arm before she could trip over it, then followed Marjorie down the stairs and out upon the drive where the others were waiting.

Hearing them, Lady Harmon came out, for she wished to see Emily go off with Lord Stearnes. Knowing that her eye was upon him, the viscount had no choice but to do as he had promised and get the girl mounted. When Emily, unable to see in which direction the horse was headed, approached timidly, he brusquely ordered her around to his side. The girl must be some sort of lack-wit, he decided, if she did not even know from which side a horse was to be mounted.

"How d'you think you'd ever get into the saddle from *that* side?" he growled, as Emily, guided by his voice, had joined him where he stood with his hands cupped to take her foot. Since Emily could not see this and did not know what she was to do, she stood waiting until he ordered, "Put your foot into my hand. No, your other one, feather-wit," and tossed her up to the horse's back. Emily felt herself thrown against the projection of the pommel and, more by accident than by design, managed to get her right foot into position, hurriedly twitching her disarranged skirt down so that she felt she was decently covered, while Arthur adjusted her stirrup to her left foot and put the reins into her hands.

The other riders, most of them already mounted, were the merest blurs to Emily. She would not have known it was the viscount who had so roughly assisted her to mount if it had not been for her mama's admonition to him to care for her. Of the group, only Lady Isobel's brightly clad figure was recognisable, and at this distance Emily could barely see that.

I shall let them ride ahead, she said to herself, and then try to keep them in sight.

She knew that the sight would be nothing more than a moving shadow ahead of her, but she must stay close enough to see them or she would certainly become lost. *Why* had not Papa come into the breakfast room when the others were talking about the hunt? He would have known, as Mama never seemed to do, how completely impossible it was for Emily to take part in something of this kind, and would have helped her to think of some way of avoiding it.

Her decision to remain behind her "hunting" companions was frustrated by her mount, which was a spirited hunter and accustomed to being in the forefront of every affair. Arthur had given the stable hands instructions to saddle this animal for her, for he sensed it was Lady Isobel's intention to make the girl appear at her worst.

It was not the sort of horse he would have ordered for her if he had known that she did not ride at all. Like the others, he believed her declaration that she did not know how to ride was an exaggeration, for everyone in his circle did so. Only when he discovered that she did not know how to mount had it occurred to him that she had been telling the truth. By that time, angry because it had seemed to him that Lady Harmon had come to make certain he kept his word to see the girl mounted, he told himself that it was too late to suggest a change. The entire hunt would be held up, and Isobel would be displeased at the delay caused by getting a tamer mount for the troublesome girl.

She ought to have had sense enough to refuse to come with us if she cannot ride, he thought to himself as he swung into his own saddle. Anyway, it would be nearly impossible for her to fall from a sidesaddle, and it wouldn't hurt her to be shaken up a bit. Doubtless Isobel would be happy when she saw the girl making a fool of herself.

At a signal, the other riders swept off to begin the chase. Emily's horse needed no urging to gallop along, trying to take what it considered its proper place near the front of the crowd.

The girl, jouncing madly in the saddle, completely forgot to hold the reins and let them drop upon the animal's neck, which it took as a signal to increase its speed. Instead, she tried to keep herself from being thrown off by gripping the edge of the saddle both before and behind her, her fingers as far beneath the leather as possible, where they were pinched unmercifully with every movement of the horse.

If they had been going more slowly, she would have tried to throw herself to earth. At this speed, however, even if she could free her right knee—which she was not certain she could do—she feared she would be badly hurt, if not killed. She might even be trampled by her horse or by one of the others that she could no longer see.

The group ahead of her poured over a low fence. Emily's mount followed, wondering why its rider had not given the proper signal but knowing what was expected of it. At the top of the jump, Emily felt that she was about to be flung from the saddle and threw herself forward onto the neck of the animal, feeling its mane beneath her fingers. This was something better to hold onto than the edge of the saddle, so she fastened both hands tightly in the hair, accidentally catching the rein lying on the right side of the horse's neck as she did so.

This was not right, the animal knew, but its rider had given a signal and it was too well trained not to obey. Without decreasing its speed, it pulled away from the others as they cleared a narrow but deep ditch, which widened considerably as it crossed Emily's path.

The horse realised the danger if its rider did not, but was unable to stop. It made a valiant effort to clear the ditch, alighting with its forefeet on solid earth, while its hindlegs vainly sought for a foothold. Finding none, it slipped backward, overbalanced, and fell inches from its rider, who had been thrown from the saddle when they were in midair.

Emily lay for several moments, half-stunned, while the animal struggled to its feet, moving disdainfully away from the object on the ground that was beginning to move, not recognising her as its former rider.

As the girl shook her head to clear it and tried to push herself upright, she was aware that someone had leapt into the ditch beside her. A quiet command to the restless horse settled it, then a pair of strong hands lifted her to her feet, steadying her.

"Are you hurt?" a deep voice asked anxiously.

"Of course I am," she wanted to say. "I am shaken half to bits and bruised from head to toe." Still, it appeared that she was in one piece with nothing broken. The stranger seemed to be concerned; and her fall had not been his fault, so she should not rail at him. "I do not think so." She was surprised that she could even speak. "I certainly ought to be, falling as I did, but—"

She broke off in confusion, realising that the man was still holding her in his arms. There was a tingling feeling deep within her that was quickly spreading to her very fingertips. It had nothing to do with what she had felt during her ride, she knew, nor with her fear, but was rather the result of being held so disturbingly close against him. She tried to draw away, but the arms that held her tightened their clasp when they felt how she was trembling. Then his mouth came down upon her own.

The world rocked madly beneath Emily's feet and hundreds of stars seemed to burst inside her. When at last he raised his head, all that she could say was, "Oh!"

"Yes," he said, as if her exclamation had made clear his sentiments as well as her own, and began kissing her again, gently at first, then more demandingly, as if he never intended to stop.

What ought she to do? Emily wondered. This man, who-ever he might be, was behaving in a most disgraceful man-ner. But what of her own behaviour? She was not only making no effort to stop the stranger from kissing her; she was also—she admitted it—enjoying his caresses.

She had heard that men—could one call them gentle-men?—sometimes acted in such a fashion, kissing girls they did not know. Still, a proper young lady ought to have screamed or swooned at such treatment. She had done neither; what must he think of her?

She made one halfhearted attempt to free herself from his embrace. Then, because his arms had pinned her own so that she could not raise them about his neck as she surprisingly found that she wished to do, she clasped them tightly about his waist and gave herself over to the wonder of his kisses. Her action caused his arms to increase the pressure of their embrace until she could scarcely breathe.

After a long, blissful moment, he said huskily, "Do you know that you have the most adorable dimples?"

"Do I?" Emily asked dreamily, ready to believe anything he said. "I did not know."

"Yes, in either cheek. There, and there." He saluted each of them, each new caress sending a thrill through her. Then his lips sought hers once more, carrying her up into a world miles and years away from Maidencourt. They were brought rudely to earth once more by a man's voice calling, "Philip, are you all right?"

The stranger quickly swept Emily from her feet and began to carry her toward a spot where he could make his way out of the ditch, calling back, "Yes—no need for anyone to worry. Miss Harmon has taken a toss, but she has not suffered any real hurt."

"Can we be of any help?"

"Thank you for the offer, but no. You might carry word to the others that I shall see Miss Harmon safely back to the house and will join you later."

"Very well, but best not make it much later," said the unseen man—unseen at least by Emily. He laughed and added, "Or you may be certain that *she* will come searching for you. You have already been missed—as you may guess—and only my assurance that I would fetch you at once has kept her to the ride."

"Make my excuses to—to everyone—if you will, and say that I shall not be long."

"Well, you have been warned," the other said and rode away, still laughing while Philip set Emily upon her feet, asking, "Do you think you will be able to ride back to the house if I lead your horse?"

"Cer-certainly." The last thing in the world that she wished to do was to mount that terrible horse once more, but she knew that she had come too far to walk, and if that was what he wished her to do. . . .

"Good girl," he said approvingly, as if he understood how reluctant she must be. He kissed her once more—a long, sweet kiss—then left her. She wondered briefly how she could get home if he did not return, but of course he would do so. Then he was at her side once more, leading the horse.

"I shall not let you fall," he assured her, lifting her into the saddle and fitting her foot into the stirrup before moving away until he was only a blur beside the horse's head. There was another shape moving beside them, which she supposed must be his horse.

They moved slowly, so she had no need to worry about falling and could spend the entire time trying to sort out her jumbled thoughts. The other man had called her rescuer "Philip," and had warned him that "she" would be searching for him. Who was *she*? Wife—sweetheart—sister —employer?

For that matter, *who* was Philip? She had not heard anyone addressed by that name during the time they had been at Maidencourt. He could be a neighbour, of course, who had ridden over to join the house party. Like Sir Hayden. No, *not* like Sir Hayden, of whom Violet had spoken with such contempt. Philip could not be contemptible, no matter how he—they—had behaved.

For all she knew, he might be the groom, who had been sent ahead to lay the trail for their hunt. A servant, and she had permitted him to kiss her. What was worse, she had returned his kisses. He must think her no better than a . . . a wanton.

Whoever he might be, whatever he might think of her, she knew that she would never forget the feel of his lips upon hers, the tingle that had gone completely through her when he touched her. Why had she not searched his face when it had been so near to her own, so that she could imprint it upon her mind, upon her heart? But her eyes had been closed during the thrill of his embrace—and might as well be closed now, since she could not see him. If they should ever meet again, she would not know him.

Not that there was much chance that they would meet again. Those moments which had been so sweet to her were doubtless no more than an instant's dalliance to him; and even if he had felt the same as she, what use was that? A man who was not acceptable in the earl's drawing room—and she had convinced herself that he would not be—would not be acceptable to her parents. She must not forget her mama's orders that she was to attract the viscount. Mama was determined that her daughter would be a countess one day and would not settle for anything less.

Emily could have wept aloud.

=10=

AS THE PAIR entered the stableyard, one of the grooms saw them and came running. Philip gave him the reins of Emily's horse, then his own, saying, "Walk my mount, but do not unsaddle him. I shall be riding out again soon."

He lifted Emily from her saddle, but, aware that the groom must be watching them, she moved quickly out of his arms with a murmur of thanks for bringing her home.

"It was my pleasure, every moment of it," he said, and Emily could feel the blood rising to her face at what she knew must be a reference to their love-making. "Come, I'll help you to the house."

That would mean that explanations would have to be made for his presence and, for all that she knew, it might be an unwelcome presence. At least as far as her mama was concerned, he would be unwelcome in her company. He must not face that on her account. Quickly, she said, "Oh please —I shall be quite all right now. It is only a short way to the house. And your . . . your friends will be waiting. You must not make them wait any longer."

"I doubt that anyone will be too greatly concerned by my absence," he said lightly. "You are certain that you do not wish me to go in with you?"

I never wished anything more, Emily thought, than to have you go with me wherever I go, forever. She wondered if his voice had really held a tender note as he asked that, or if she had only imagined it because she wished for it. How she longed to have him take her in his arms once more, to feel his lips upon hers—as shameless as such a longing must be.

Still, even if she could not see the groom, she could hear the sound of the horse's hooves as he was walked about and knew the man was nearby. She was certain that Philip, for all his earlier behaviour, was too much a gentleman to act so rashly before a servant. Also, she remembered—like a knife thrust—that the other rider had told Philip that *she* would be waiting for him.

"No, no, I shall be quite all right now that I am here." On no account must he be allowed to get into trouble—more trouble—because of her. "You have been most kind to bring me this far, and I thank you for what you have done."

She began to blush again as it occurred to her that he might think that she was thanking him for having kissed her. That was not what she had meant, but secretly she thanked him for that as well. Philip could not fail to be aware of her confusion and caught both her hands in his, pressing them lightly as he said, "No thanks are necessary. It was my good fortune to be there at the moment and to be able to come to your aid. And if there is nothing more that I can do for you, I shall bid you farewell—for the moment."

Emily could not see him accept his horse from the groom and ride away, but she could hear his hoofbeats in the distance before she moved. The groom caught her before she could walk into the stable wall, and headed her in the direction of the house.

Watching her erratic path, he wondered if her tumble might have addled her brain and whether he ought to see her into the care of someone who could look after her. Then he shrugged and went about his own work. It was not his duty, after all, to look after Quality, only after their horses.

"And what possessed a little thing like that to be trying to ride Thunderer is beyond me," he said, going over the animal carefully to make certain that *it* had suffered no damage in the fall. For all that her son had ordered it for the lady, the countess would have his hide if her favourite animal was harmed.

Emily made the journey to the house almost without incident. Once she collided with a tree and another time sprawled upon a croquet wicket that a servant had overlooked, but such accidents were normal to her. Besides, she had too much on her mind to think of where she might be going.

Nor was she the only one. As he rode to rejoin his friends, the duke had time to wonder at his own behaviour. It was not his habit to go about making love to innocent young ladies. Such actions he left to rakes like Barham.

He had his share of *affaires*, of course. That was a different matter entirely. His companions in these adventures knew what they were about. And if a pretty girl came into his arms in a provocative situation—usually one that she had contrived—he might kiss her lightly *once*, but no more than that.

The Harmon chit and the toss she had taken had given him concern. Still, that scarcely excused his subsequent behaviour. His first kiss had been intended to soothe a frightened child, but he had discovered that it was no child he held in his arms, who had returned his kisses with such fervour.

Looking at what had happened from another view, could the accident, which naturally could well have overset even an experienced rider, have been responsible for the manner in which she had accepted his embraces? More than that, the manner in which she had returned them? Or might it have been that the chit was more experienced than she had seemed and was merely taking advantage of the situation?

"If she reports the matter to her parents, which she doubtless will do," he confided to his horse, who responded to the familiar voice with a flick of its ears, "I can expect Lord Harmon to descend upon me, breathing fire and demanding to know my intentions toward his daughter. Lord, wouldn't *that* send Isobel into the boughs.''

Durban considered that he was as knowledgeable in the ways of females as any man, perhaps more knowledgeable than most. Yet the girl's actions were bewildering in every way. Almost any other girl he had met would have pretended to be dismayed by his actions, fluttering her eyelashes (and what pretty eyelashes the little Harmon had, he found himself thinking) at him and saying, ''Oh, Your Grace—'' or ''Your Grace, you should not—'' even as she mentally added up the advantages of having taken his interest.

The little Harmon, however, had employed none of the usual stratagems. This must be a new ploy, one he had never encountered, and he thought he knew them all. The girl behaved as if she had not realised the possible advantages of the situation. It was almost as if she had not known who he was.

As if she had not. . . . Pondering over that fact, which seemed impossible considering the number of encounters they had had, he recalled several incidents of the past few days. The girl had told them that she did not ride, and her awkwardness in handling the horse, allowing him to run off from the others, made it seem that she was telling the truth.

Then there were other things: the way she had tripped upon General Allenby's cane and spilt the tea over Isobel. Yesterday, she had nearly walked into the path of the racing horses and, last evening, in her flight, she had collided with him in the doorway. She was frightened, but one would have thought she had not seen him.

Philip began to grin. ''That is the answer, of course,'' he told his mount. ''She could *not* see. The girl has been running about Maidencourt like a bat at noonday, unable to see what is right before her eyes.''

That meant that she had no idea who had been kissing her and that there would be no repercussions upon that score. Since she had not known that he was the duke, was it he,

Philip Leslie, who had evoked that response—or would she have responded with the same eagerness no matter who the man had been? If that were so, it meant the girl was fast and that he might put the incident entirely out of his mind.

Irrationally, he found that he was slightly disappointed to think that the matter could be put aside so easily. It should not matter, since the episode would never be repeated, but he *wanted* to believe that he was the only one who could evoke that response from her.

By the time he had reached his friends, the mock hunt had been ended and they were on their way back to the house. It should have continued for some time; he was certain that it was Isobel who had cut it short, and he was aware of how her green eyes sparkled with anger as he joined her. Isobel was not accustomed to being deserted, even for a short time, and even if there were plenty of company at hand. Certainly not so that her chosen escort could go to the rescue of another girl.

"Well, Durban," she asked, and the sweetness she tried to put into her tone was not enough to hide the acid which lay beneath it, "did you get the tiresome child back to her nurse?"

You would be greatly surprised, my lady, the duke thought, stifling a smile, if you knew how far from being a child the little Harmon actually is. However, this was something best forgot. More to the point was Isobel's attitude. As the days went by, he was becoming more and more aware of the change that came over Isobel's features when she made such remarks as this. It was not a change for the better. Nonetheless, his voice was as pleasant as ever when he said, "Do you know, Isobel, you will become a complete shrew if you do not take care?"

That young sapskull, Arthur, who had been riding as close at her ladyship's side as their mounts would permit, bristled at this disparagement of his ideal. Philip was such a dry old stick that he had never appreciated this wonderful creature properly, he thought. After all, it was not *Isobel* who was to blame for the hunt being curtailed.

Lady Isobel, however, had been jolted by Durban's words into the realisation that she might have gone too far this time. She was *almost* certain that he would offer for her, yet he had left her nearly alone while he went knight-erranting off to rescue a nursery brat.

Still, it was no part of her plan to do anything at this stage of the game which might antagonise him. He would pay dearly for having made that comment about her temper, but not until she had his wedding ring safely upon her finger. Forcing a light laugh, she said, "I only meant that it *was* tiresome of her to spoil our hunt. And such an obvious thing for her to have done, too—trying to attract your attention by falling off her horse in that manner, knowing that you would be forced to stop and help her."

Clever indeed of the little nuisance, Isobel thought. Who would have imagined she would be that cunning? But if she thought that she was going to be allowed to get away with such a scheme, she must think again. Her ladyship had no intention of allowing a valuable catch like the duke to wander.

Philip thought for a moment of telling her that he was almost certain that, even now, Emily had not the least idea who her rescuer had been, but decided that there was no reason for giving away her secret. To some of his friends and most of all, he was positive, to Isobel, the fact that the girl could not see what was going on about her would be a cause for further laughter and doubtless some cruel jokes at her expense. She did not deserve such treatment.

"I doubt if there was anything about the accident which was planned," he said instead, "for she could not have been certain that I—or anyone else—could have seen her fall, as far from us as she had gone. Rather, I believe that she had lost control of her horse. The fault lies with the person who provided such a spirited mount as Thunderer for a young lady who had already told us that she was unaccustomed to riding. It was you, I suppose, halfling."

He fixed an accusing eye upon his cousin, who began to bluster, but who was careful not to say anything to give the duke the idea that he had hoped to please Isobel by providing so unruly a horse. She had not actually *asked* him to do so; it was only that he had felt that was what she would like. And Philip was already critical enough of Isobel because of the actions of that stupid little friend of Violet's.

"How was I to know that she really did not ride? I thought it was merely a disclaimer, to make us urge her to go, for of course everyone rides. Although, now that I come to think of it, she *was* awkward in mounting. It seemed to me almost as if she did not know from which side she was to get into the saddle."

"And even with such evidence as that before you, it did not occur to you that she truly did not know how to ride —that it would be best if you saw to it that she had a better-tempered animal? Arthur, I always knew you to be a clunch, but I never realised until this moment just how buffle-headed you really are."

His tone was so scornful of the younger man that Lady Isobel was moved to protest. "Really, Durban, you are being much too hard upon the boy." Arthur winced at the word "boy," which he considered derogatory to one who had reached his majority more than a month past, and especially when it made it appear that his adored one held him to be of little account. "*I* believe he had no idea that anything was amiss, that he was only trying to be kind to that troublesome girl."

She believed nothing of the sort; it was clear to her that the young man had wished to please her by making the girl look foolish. He had not thought that she might be hurt, and it seemed that she had not been.

Her ladyship was seething with anger, however. Instead of

becoming disgusted with that Harmon chit as he ought to have done, for behaving as she did and ruining their sport, Durban had actually gone to help her. Now he was berating poor Arthur on her account, when it was entirely the girl's fault; if she could not manage the horse she had been given, she ought to have said so at once.

Seeing the glitter in Isobel's eyes and Arthur's sulky expression, Philip sighed and gave over the idea of making either of them view the matter sensibly. "Very well," he said, "I'll grant him that much. Now, shall we forget the incident?"

The others were more than willing—at least, outwardly —to do so, especially those who were closest to him, and the party rode back to the house chatting of other matters. Despite the fact that he had been the one to make the suggestion, however, the duke found that he was unable to forget what had happened. He smiled as he recalled the pleasure of holding the little Harmon in his arms, the feel of her lips responding to his kisses.

He frowned so suddenly that Arthur shot uneasy glances at him, wondering if Philip had thought of some other reason to blame him or, what was worse, to blame Isobel for some imagined wrong. The duke's thoughts, however, were still with the young lady he had rescued. *Was* she fast, he wondered, or had she merely been so overset by the toss she had taken that her reaction was almost an hysterical one? Or was it a reaction of relief that she had escaped unharmed, as his had been—in the beginning?

Still, she had not known who he was; he was almost certain of that. The matter could be put from his mind, for she would not be expecting more attention from him. Then why had he not forgot it already; why must he keep telling himself to do so?

It seemed to him that Isobel had been pleased that the younger girl had fallen from her horse. Doubtless she still resented the incident of the spilt tea. It had been an expensive gown which had been spoilt; he was sure of that. Isobel made a habit of dressing beyond the limits of her purse.

He would offer to replace the gown. That should turn her up sweet once more. It would not be the first bill he had paid for her ladyship—nor would it be the last. As his duchess—if he decided to offer for her, as it seemed likely he would do—she would most certainly cost him a great deal. Still, he could afford it.

The flashes of temper she was showing more frequently these days were a different matter, and one which was much less pleasant than his ability to dress his wife elegantly. If she could not learn to control them, their life together would be most disagreeable. Unbidden, a memory of large, pansy-coloured eyes and soft, trembling lips came into his mind, but he put it ruthlessly aside. At nearly seven-and-twenty, he should be well past the age of romantic daydreams.

Emily, meanwhile, had made her way to her room, remembering not to curtsy to the suit of armour guarding the stairs, although the impulse to repeat her first day's error recurred each time she saw the shadowy figure. If someone was in the hall and saw her, she might be thought a bit—well, a bit odd. She contented herself with once more touching the mailed shoulder lightly as she passed.

With the door of her room closed carefully behind her, she located the oblongs of white that must be the windows and, skirting the furniture which loomed in her way, gained a casement and knelt with her arms folded upon the sill.

She was not able to see the magnificent view that spread before her, but at the moment it did not matter. The scent of many flowers rose from the lawn below, and she wished for a time that she could hear the birds chirping, as she would have been able to do at Harmon Hall, instead of the screeching noise that came from somewhere below. Bird songs would be better suited to her present mood.

131

There were no peacocks at Harmon Hall, so Emily was unfamiliar with their noise and for several moments thought
idly that she ought to fetch her spectacles so that she could
discover what was causing so much clamour. Somehow, it did
not seem as important for her to know this as she usually felt
about things. Before long she could not hear it or anything
else except for the deep voice saying, "You have the most
adorable dimples."

"Do I?" she murmured as she had done before, touching
the spot on either cheek that Philip's lips had brushed. As
she felt the indentations she had not known were there, she
smiled to think that they had pleased him.

Letting her fingers slide across her lip , she wondered anew
at the sensations that had gone through her at his embrace,
his kisses. In common with every other young lady who had
perused the romances that lay between the marbled covers
identifying the products of the Minerva Press, Emily had
frequently felt herself akin to the heroines who swooned in
the arms of the personable heroes.

It was strange, but she had felt no inclination at all to
swoon when she was in Philip's arms. His kisses had swept
her up into a wonderful world which she had not been able
to imagine, but her only wish had been that the happiness
might go on forever.

Resting her cheek upon her folded arms, she half-
whispered, "Philip." Could any other name be half so wonderful as that one? Its very sound conjured up the memory of
strong arms holding her close, of lips caressing her.

"What did you say?" Lady Harmon asked sharply from
the doorway.

Turning quickly in the direction of the accusing voice,
Emily overbalanced and sprawled upon the floor.

"I—I did not hear you come in," she stammered, trying
to push herself back up to her knees.

"It is evident that you did not." The sight of her daughter
lying upon the floor drove the fact that her question had not

been answered out of Lady Harmon's mind. She had thought her safely in the viscount's care, only to find her here.

"What, may I ask, do you think you are doing, lying about here like a wanton when you should be out where Stearnes can see you? You cannot expect him to come *here* after you."

"The others are riding." She had not heard their return, so it was safe to assume they were still out.

"Then why did you not go with them? I told you that you should do so, and I saw you put up on the horse myself."

"Yes, I know; I did try to go. Or at least I started. But you know that I never learnt to ride, Mama, so of course I could not keep up with the others. My horse ran away and threw me, so I had to come back to the house."

Pray that Mama did not think to ask if anyone had helped her when she had fallen or had shown her the way back. She could not bear to speak to anyone about Philip, especially not to Mama, who would never understand and would scold her unmercifully for her behaviour. If Mama thought she looked like a wanton merely because she had fallen to the floor, what would she think if she knew about those moments spent in Philip's arms?

Lady Harmon, however, had accepted the story without question, her mind upon other matters much more important to her.

"I suppose that accounts for your looking like a scullery maid," she said, casting a scornful eye upon the muddied habit, "but not for your lying about here. Get up from the floor, do, and get yourself into something becoming before they return. The pink, I believe; you do look fetching in pink, and Stearnes is certain to approve. Shall I send Hough to help you?"

The offer of her own dresser was a supreme concession upon her part, but nothing was too much if it helped to establish her daughter as a future countess.

"Oh no, Mama, thank you." Emily scrambled to her feet,

hoping that she was looking in the direction of her mama and not at the bedpost. Mama always disliked it if she thought Emily was not paying her the proper attention. "I know you will wish her services, and Spence helps me very well. It was so thoughtful of Violet to let me have her."

She would not say so, but she much preferred the services of the sympathetic Spence to those of Hough, that superior being who seemed to share her mistress's belief that Emily *could* see if she would only make the effort to do so.

"Very well, I shall leave you now, so ring for the woman and see that she makes you look your prettiest. Emily, you do not seem to realise how important it is for you to make more of an effort. We have only a few days before we must leave here. If you have not succeeded in capturing Lord Stearnes's interest before we go, you can hardly expect him to follow you. And it may be a long time before you have another opportunity as grand as this one. You should know that heirs to earldoms are not to be found on every corner."

"Yes, Mama," Emily said obediently, fighting back an impulse to burst into tears, for her mama would never understand. She could not see that the viscount had never paid the least attention to Emily—and the girl wished with all her heart that he would not.

Still, it was her duty to marry sometime, and life as Lady Stearnes—even if her husband always ignored her—would be far preferable to a lifetime of listening to Mama bewail her lost chances.

═11═

LUNCHEON THAT DAY was a festive meal. Most of the riders had enjoyed the mock hunt, despite the fact that it had been cut short, and their praise of Lady Isobel for having been the instigator of such a diversion was so high that she was well pleased with the world.

Bribed by the duke with the offer of a new gown to replace the one which had been spoilt—and in the mistaken belief that he would be none the wiser if she encouraged the dressmaker to increase the bill to cover the price of several items already long outstanding on her account—she had paused beside Emily's chair to say, "I trust, Miss Harmon, that you find yourself none the worse for your spill?"

"Oh no, thank you, Lady Isobel," Emily said, getting to her feet, happy that her ladyship was no longer angry with her, but Lady Isobel had passed on without waiting for a reply and ignored her for the balance of the meal. Even to please Durban, there was a limit to how kind she ought to be to a child who was troublesome and—she recalled the spilt tea—extremely dangerous.

Once more, again by Violet's machinations, Emily found herself being escorted to the table by the viscount. That young gentleman, however, was still smarting under the set-down which his cousin had administered during the ride and, from the moment they were seated, ignored all of Emily's timid conversational gambits, or replied, when it was necessary for him to do so, with a curtness that repelled her.

Arthur toyed with his food, glowering across the table at the duke and wishing that he, instead of Philip, had been placed beside Isobel. *He* would appreciate her properly, as it was clear that Philip did not. And blast Violet for saddling him again with this obnoxious chit. Was he never to be rid of her during the party?

From time to time, as he responded to Isobel's chatter, trying to turn the conversation into other channels whenever it threatened to become as intimate as Isobel wished it to be, the duke glanced across the table at his heir. He must marry soon, he thought, if only to make certain that young idiot Arthur was not to step into his shoes one day.

There he sat, sulking like a schoolboy because of some well-deserved criticism of his thoughtlessness and paying no attention to his luncheon partner. He owed the girl at least an apology for having provided her with such a mount this morning. The little Harmon seemed to be slightly worried at being so ignored, as well she might be, but he was happy to note that she appeared to be none the worse for her tumble. He smiled as he recalled the aftermath of the rescue, then pushed the thought aside and scowled at Arthur.

Emily did indeed look her best, thanks to Spence's ministrations. The abigail had helped her to bathe, and had put her into a gown that was—as the earl commented —exactly the colour of a blush rose. There were rows of fine lace about the bodice and down the full short sleeves. She had also arranged the girl's hair in an artless style that became her, fastened back on either side with small bows of pink to match her gown, and had wrested from her the black slipper she had been about to put on and had given her instead the mate to the pink kid one she had already donned.

Gathering up the discarded habit, she had, upon seeing its condition, at first exclaimed, "Tcha!" then had said encouragingly, "It's not so bad, after all, miss, truly. It hasn't been torn, and I'll see that it is cleaned and pressed properly before returning it to Miss Allenby.''

She looked at the girl critically, asking—as Lady Harmon had failed to do—''I hope you were not hurt when you fell?''

Assuring her that she had suffered nothing more than fright—''and that from the moment I was put on the horse's back''—and some unimportant bruises, Emily confided the story of her unfortunate attempt to ride. Even to Spence's sympathetic ear, however, she did not tell its sequel. Those wonderful moments, shameless though they might have been, were much too precious to be shared with anyone.

Spence could hardly fail to note the girl's blushes and drew her own conclusions, only partially correct. She was right in thinking that there must be a gentleman involved in the adventure, one whom the young lady did not wish to mention. To her mind, Miss Harmon was prettier than any of the other ladies in the house party, and she hoped that the gentleman, whoever he might be, would think the same. Having been with the family for many years, she had no great opinion of the viscount. The worst she could say of him, however, was that he was a lack-wit and totally selfish, so she hoped that it was he, and not that rakish Sir John.

That one will break Lady Violet's heart or I miss my guess, she said to herself. I wouldn't want him to hurt this little lady, too. Lady Violet will recover more easily than this one.

She did not think for a moment that it might be one of Lord Stearnes's friends who had captured Miss Harmon's interest. As far as she knew, neither of them seemed to be much in the petticoat line; she had not had a chance to observe the glances that Mr. Gillian was casting in Lady Violet's direction these days. As for the young lady, Spence doubted that she had noticed either of them. So it must be either the viscount or Sir John.

For a time she wondered if she should give the girl a word of caution about the older man's reputation, for it seemed to her that Lady Harmon—with her eyes fixed firmly on the possibility of a match between her daughter and Lord Stearnes—had not noticed the change in Miss Emily since the morning's outing.

No, I'd best say nothing, Spence warned herself. 'Tis not my place to advise her, much as I like the young lady. Anyhow, when they leave here, Sir John—if that is who it is—won't be welcome to follow her home.

So she had said nothing, and Emily had gone down to luncheon to try to obey her mama's orders and fix Lord Stearnes's interest, although she would have preferred to stay in her room and dream of Philip. With every minute she sat at the luncheon table, it was more certain to her that she was failing miserably in her task. How could she fix his interest when she could not even gain it?

Although she could not see them, the girl was aware of the frowns Lady Harmon must be sending her way. *Why* did the girl not make a better effort, her ladyship asked herself over and over as the meal progressed. She did not wish Emily to flirt, precisely, but there were any number of ways in which a clever girl could draw a gentleman's attention to herself.

When they were alone, she would speak to Emily more sharply, impress upon her the importance of making this match. She thought she had already got that through Emily's head, but it seemed that she had not, from the way in which the girl let every opportunity slip by—opportunities which existed only in her ladyship's mind, of course.

Violet, who had finally been forced to the conclusion which Lady Harmon would not yet face—that, pretty as Emily might be, she had no chance of drawing Arthur's attention away from Lady Isobel—came to Emily's side when luncheon was finished, to coax her to come for a drive with herself and the other young ladies.

"No, I thank you," Emily replied, close to tears at the knowledge that she was failing her mama. "I think I had best return to my room. A migraine—" She broke off, recalling that she had already used that excuse upon another occasion.

Violet remembered it as well and caught herself on the verge of saying, "What, another one?" Then she thought of the morning's happenings and exclaimed instead, "Of course; I do not wonder that you have one. What a dreadful experience that must have been for you."

Having been in the forefront of the hunt, enjoying it despite the fact that it had been Isobel's idea, she had not heard of Emily's mishap until the duke had rejoined the party. She had wanted to run to Emily's side as soon as they had returned to the house, but had been forced to dress for luncheon. The earl, good-natured at most times, was inclined to become quite testy if anyone—especially one of the family—made it necessary for him to delay the start of any meal. A little thing like a toss from a horse would be no excuse in his eyes; everyone took a toss now and then. He might have been willing to overlook Emily's absence, since she was the one who had been thrown, but his daughter had no such excuse.

Emily had looked so fit when she came to the table that her friend had been reassured. Still, she had heard of cases where the full effects of such an event did not become felt for some time. Apparently, that was what had happened to Emily. The poor girl was certainly suffering the aftereffects of her accident.

"Is there anything I can bring you?" Violet asked anxiously.

Emily shook her head. "No—if only I might rest for a time."

It was not *entirely* a lie, Emily thought as she made her way slowly up the stairs to her room, too deep in her problem to pay attention to Sir Edmund's armour. Certainly she was not suffering from a migraine, but she had no name to give to the sickly nervous churning feeling within her when she thought of what her mama would have to say to her. She knew now that, no matter how much time she was given, she would never be able to attract the viscount, and in her mama's eyes she would be forever a failure, one who did not have the wit to take advantage of the opportunities that were—her mama seemed to think—placed before her.

She would be safe enough in her room from Violet and her friends as long as they thought her making a recovery from the effects of her tumble. Lady Harmon, however, would be at her side the moment she heard that Emily had once more slipped away instead of following the viscount about.

Mama's anger would have to be faced sooner or later, but in a fashion she knew to be cowardly, Emily preferred to delay the meeting as long as possible. Catching up the reticule, which held her spectacles, she slipped out of the room once more. In a shadowed corner of the hallway, she stopped to don her spectacles and to look about her carefully to make certain that there was no one to see her as she stole down the stairs, again ignoring Sir Edmund's armour, and went out onto the terrace.

For the first time, she could see the lake, which had aroused her mama's admiration on the day they arrived, and as she followed the walk that led toward the lake, she could see the white spot upon the far hill, which must be the folly. She thought for several moments of going to examine it, for she had never seen anything of that sort, but she could not be certain that she would not be spied by some far-sighted person at the house, and she wished to be alone for a time.

To her right stretched a wooded patch that, as far as she could tell, was much larger than the spinney growing near Harmon Hall. Of course, everything here was larger than at home, she thought as she took the path that led among the trees. She lost all track of the time she spent walking along, stopping now and then to examine the tracery of a leaf or the shape of a young tree. How wonderful it was to be able to *see* things. She wondered if people who had always been able to see well realised how fortunate they were.

A small hare skittered across her path, startling her at first, then making her laugh. "Come back," she called after it. "I shall not hurt you." But it was out of sight.

A dell filled with gently swaying blossoms caught her eyes, and she left the path to go nearer to it. She did not recognise them as windflowers, but admired their delicate beauty. Feeling tired from her unaccustomed walk after the excitement of the morning, she sat down upon the grass, her back against a small tree, watching the movements of the flowers and wishing she might find some way of averting her mama's anger at her failure to snare the viscount.

Here, however, among all these beautiful things, such matters did not seem to be important. Half-mesmerised by the swaying flowers, she found herself remembering instead the strength of Philip's arms about her, the magic of his lips upon hers.

The deep rumble of thunder and the "splat" of raindrops striking upon the leaves around her woke her, and she leapt to her feet. Here where the trees grew so thickly, she could not see how the clouds had piled up overhead while she dozed, but a lightning flash was visible, and the sharp thunderclap that accompanied it told her she would soon be soaked if she did not return to the house at once.

Hurrying up the hill to the path, she started walking in the direction she thought she had come, but the path soon began twisting and turning among the trees in an unfamiliar way. She must have come the wrong way, she thought, and she turned back in an effort to find the flower-filled dell. Another path crossed the one she was following, and she hesitated. Had she come along this path or the one directly ahead? Following one path, then another, she knew now that she was completely lost.

"And no one knows where I am," she moaned, darting

off in a new direction, her panic mounting as she tripped over roots, and bushes caught at her gown and scratched her hands. "I might be here for days—or forever."

At the house, as the servants closed windows and fastened shutters against the unexpected storm, a young groom approached, although he was not supposed to be in the house at this time. Seeing the butler directing the labours of several footmen, he went to him and asked anxiously, "Did the young lady get back all right?"

Dobbs gave him a look which was intended to impress him with the fact that his place was in the stables and not at the house, and that he should remain in his own area unless he was summoned here. The young man, however, ignored the look and stubbornly stood his ground, awaiting an answer to his question.

"What lady do you mean?" Dobbs asked haughtily, loath to think that one of the servants might know more of the workings of Maidencourt than he. "And back from where?" And what business is it of yours, he wanted to add, but thought it beneath his dignity.

"I dunno who she be, but she come from the house and I noticed her goin' into the woods some hours ago."

Dobbs could not imagine that any of the ladies would be so lost to propriety as to be walking in the woods unescorted—or, worse still, to be walking there *with* an escort. Most likely, it had been one of the maids slipping out to meet a swain, and if he discovered which of them was guilty, she would be severely reprimanded for neglecting her duties.

"If it was that long ago, she certainly must have returned by this time," said Dobbs.

"I never noticed her comin' back." Then, because he knew that Dobbs was about to tell him that he had no right to be neglecting his work to look after an errant female—not that he had to answer to the butler for his actions—he said quickly, "A'corse, I was workin' and coulda missed her."

"Doubtless that is exactly what happened, and I suggest that you return to your work unless you wish to be of help here," Dobbs said in a tone which dismissed him.

The man hurried off, glad that he worked under the head groom, who was almost human, and not under that "stiff-rumped fellow," as he privately labelled the butler. Certainly that one could not be expected to be concerned about anyone who might be lost in the woods in this storm. Pulling his collar up about his ears, he dashed to the shelter of the stables, hoping that the young lady *had* returned.

Although he had sent the groom off with a flea in his ear, Dobbs did not put the matter out of his mind. He immediately sought out the housekeeper to discover which of the girls had slipped out when she should have been working. No such loose behaviour could be permitted at Maidencourt as long as he was in charge of the staff, and the girl involved could expect the severest reprimand, and if she was as saucy as some of the younger ones were these days, she would be turned off.

He said as much to the housekeeper and was met with a burst of indignation. He could be certain that it had not been one of *her* girls who had been roaming about.

"I know where each one of them is every minute of the day—*and* the night," Mrs. Johnson declared, drawing herself up like a pouter pigeon. "Do you think I'd do otherwise when we have a rake staying in the house, not to mention a pair of young snirps who would like to follow his example, or I miss my guess. It's been making no end of extra work for us, but either I or one of my older girls has had the young ones under her eye every minute."

Dobbs, of course, was above Mrs. Johnson in the hierarchy of the servants' hall, but he had good reason to know her temper. When roused, as it was at this moment, the smooth running of the household could be disrupted. Quickly, he apologised for having doubted her watchfulness for a moment and made his escape, hoping that she would not fume too long over what she considered to be an insult.

So it had not been one of the maids whom the groom had seen—if he had seen anyone at all. Could one of the young ladies have been slipping out alone, or to meet someone? He was not the arbiter of *their* morals, he thought thankfully, but what if one of them should have been caught out in the storm?

He pondered for some time, trying to decide whether his duty lay in reporting the matter or in turning a blind eye upon the escapades of the Quality. At last, hoping that he had made the right choice, he went in search of the earl, finding him in his study going over some estate matters with his nephew. The earl, his normally good humour considerably disturbed at having to take advice from someone who—although he might be the head of the family, was almost young enough to be his son—was inclined to dismiss the butler's report as unworthy of his concern.

"All these gels are flighty," he announced. "Nothing like they were in my day when a lady behaved like a lady."

Repressing an impulse to say that he had heard plenty of stories to belie that statement, the duke suggested, "Still, considering the storm, might it not be a good idea to make certain that she—whoever she might be—has returned to the house safely? It would be a bad thing if something happened to one of your guests."

There he went again, giving unwanted advice. Why, the earl thought testily, did his brother have to be so unreasonable as to die and leave this *youngster* as the family head? After all, *he* had made his way up to an earldom with no—well, with very little—family influence. Durban ought to respect his ability as well as his age. But did he? If so, he certainly gave no evidence of it.

"Oh, very well," he said ungraciously, and gave the order to see that all the guests were in the house, certain that this would be a waste of time. Might as well show Durban, however, that he did not know everything.

All of the young—and not so young—ladies were quickly located in one of the drawing rooms. The girls were gossiping, their mothers doing the same, although they would angrily have denied having their conversation described in that manner. The countess was deep in conversation with Lady Harmon, who was beginning to wonder if she was going to have to go and fetch Emily down to the viscount's side.

Lady Isobel was sulking because the duke had deserted her and she had no better company than the fawning viscount. She went to Durban's side the moment he arrived, but her attempts to draw him into a tête-à-tête were ignored.

Only Emily Harmon was missing from the group, and her mama looked up from the *on-dits*, which had been claiming only a fraction of her attention as Violet replied to the duke's question, saying that her friend had gone to her room, not feeling well after the morning's accident.

Only another excuse to keep from doing as she should, her ladyship said to herself, planning to take the girl sharply to task for not doing as she had been told.

"Will you see if she is there?" Philip asked, and Violet, always willing to oblige her cousin, ran upstairs herself rather than sending a servant. She was back in a moment or two to report that Emily was not there.

"Then she may have been the one the groom reported that he saw going into the woods and, if so, she is doubtless lost out there in the storm," Durban told her. Not Emily, something within him was saying. *She* must not be lost.

Violet shrieked in dismay at the thought of her friend being lost, and her cry was echoed by several members of the party. The two who showed the least reaction were Lady Harmon and Lady Isobel. Lady Harmon was somewhat worried about her daughter, but she could not help thinking that it was exactly like Emily to be wandering about somewhere when she should be here attempting to win Lord Stearnes.

"One might know that it would be that troublesome girl who is lost. She has been nothing but a disaster since she arrived," said Lady Isobel spitefully.

"Isobel, you are nothing but a mean old . . . cat," Violet cried, bursting into tears. "Emily is my *friend*, and she may be in danger."

Lady Harmon shot an angry glance at Violet, but said nothing. She did not feel that it was proper for her to contradict the daughter of an earl, even in defense of her own daughter; also, Lady Isobel was right. Emily had caused a great deal of trouble in the short time they had been at Maidencourt. The duke, on the other hand, gave Isobel a look that warned her to make no further comments. "We must begin a search for her at once," he ordered. Disregarding the fact that this was his uncle's house and not his own, Philip began to organise the servants and the younger men of the party to beat the woods. If he waited for the earl to take charge, who knew what might happen to the girl? Who knew, in fact, what might already have happened to her?

The poor child, he thought, out in this weather, and she must certainly be lost. Blind as a bat, too. What could have possessed her to go off in such a manner?

Despite the fact that she was wearing her spectacles, Emily was in almost as sorry a plight as the duke imagined her to be. The sky had darkened with the advent of the storm, and enough rain had made its way through the trees to coat her spectacles with water until she could see little farther through them than without them. She tried to wipe them but only succeeded in smearing the glass. Then, too, other rain continued to fall on them as she plunged first along one path, then another. At last, for lack of breath to run farther, she stopped, clinging to a tree and sobbing.

"No one will ever find me," she wailed. "I shall go on wandering about here until I die."

She might as well give up and die at once, she thought, sinking to the earth, then struggling to her feet again as she imagined that she had heard someone call her name. She held her breath, listening until the call came again. When she tried to reply, her voice was only a croak, but her second attempt was better.

"Stay where you are and keep answering me," the voice ordered. Emily obeyed, wishing to hurry in his direction, but not having enough breath both to run and shout. When the man came in sight, she released her hold upon the tree and clung to him instead, remembering just in time to snatch off her spectacles and keep them hidden in her hand; her reticule had long since been lost.

Her rescuer impatiently freed one arm from her grasp and raised the hunting horn he carried, blowing a blast that made Emily's head ring. It had been the duke's idea to outfit the members of the search party with various means of attracting the attention of others when—he would not permit himself to say "if"—Emily was found, and one of the horns had been given to Lord Stearnes.

The viscount had taken positive pleasure in the way Emily had winced when he blew the horn almost in her ear. The chit could consider herself fortunate, he thought, that he was not carrying a pistol as his cousin was doing. Instead of firing into the air, he would have been tempted to put a bullet into her for this escapade. His favourite hunting coat had been ripped upon a thorn bush, and he doubted that his man would ever be able to restore his Hessians to their former brilliance. And she was to blame for all of this just because she had no better sense than to lose herself in the wood.

"Too bad she could not remain lost," he muttered savagely.

Moving away, more from dislike than from any desire to protect her ears from the noise, he blew several more sharp blasts and heard some of the others call in answer. It had been decided—ordered by Philip, actually—that only the one who found Emily was to signal other than by voice, to avoid confusion.

Some of the others were now approaching, shouting congratulations to the fortunate hunter. Arthur caught Emily's hand, dragging her toward them and growling, "Come along; maybe we can get back to the house before this rig of mine is completely ruined."

===12===

As Spence, keeping up a soothing murmur of "poor chick," and similar expressions, pried the spectacles from Emily's cold fingers, then helped her out of her torn and muddied gown and hurried her into a hot bath, Lady Harmon bustled into the room. Unable to see her mama's face, Emily tried to shrink farther into the tub, bracing herself for the scold she expected to receive because of her imprudence in wandering off and becoming lost.

To her surprise, Lady Harmon said nothing; Emily could not see how she busied herself with picking up and putting down various objects in the room until Spence had bundled Emily into a warm robe and tucked her into bed. Then her ladyship, waving the abigail away, came to seat herself on the side of her daughter's bed, clasping both of her hands.

"My dear child," she said in a tone that was so warm it made Emily blink. "What a wonderful piece of good fortune this is. I was prepared to be quite angry with you, but it has certainly all turned out for the best."

"It has?" For some reason that she could not understand, she was not to be scolded.

"You foolish child, of course it has. I must admit I did not think you were so clever, but how in the world did you manage it so that it was the viscount who found you?"

So that was who the gentleman had been. From the way he had dragged her along and growled at her, Emily did not believe that *he* had thought it was fortunate. In fact, he had appeared to be quite infuriated with her. "I . . . did not manage it. It only happened that way."

"It does not matter. The result is the same." She almost smothered Emily in her embrace, then sat back and looked at her critically. "You do look a bit fagged out, as George would say. I think it might be best for you to have a tray in your room. I shall make your excuses; no one will expect you, for everyone will understand that you have been through an ordeal. But come down later and make your thanks to Lord Stearnes for coming to your rescue. Nothing so impresses a gentleman as to know that a lady thinks him a hero. Especially if she looks at him soulfully as she thanks him. Now, mind you, do as I say and we—you—will have him yet."

She patted her daughter's damp hair and went out of the room, humming happily if decidedly off-key, already planning the details of Emily's wedding. When the door had closed behind her, Spence came from the far side of the room, where she had been waiting, carrying a large towel. After she had rubbed the girl's head vigorously, she tucked the blankets more firmly about her.

"I'll have one of the maids bring your dinner," she announced. "Then you must try to get some sleep."

"Oh no—I mean, I would like the tray, thank you, Spence, for I am quite hungry, but Mama wishes for me to go downstairs afterward."

Spence shook her head disapprovingly. It should be clear to anyone that what the young lady needed after such a harrowing experience as she had undergone was plenty of rest and coddling. She would get no coddling from her ladyship, Spence thought grimly, and precious little rest, either. Still, she had given her orders, and it was unlikely that Miss Harmon would disobey.

"Rest as long as you can, then," she said. "I'll be back to help you dress." There was no way of telling how the girl might rig herself out if someone did not look after her.

Thinking of the time she had tried to wear one pink and one black slipper, Spence shook her head once more.

She had grown fond of the young lady in the few days she had been serving her, but she also pitied her just as she pitied her sister Sukey. It only went to show, she thought, how little the people knew who said that money could buy everything. Miss Harmon was well-enough inlaid, if not precisely swimming in lard, and still she could not find her way across the room without help.

The incident of the tea spilling had been discussed more than once in the servants' hall, but Spence was certain that she was the only one who knew the true reason for it. Lady Isobel's dresser, who was a haughty individual much disliked by the Maidencourt servants, had hinted strongly that she believed it to have been done purposely. At last her version had been accepted by the others, and Miss Harmon was considered by many of them as something of a heroine for having doused her ladyship. Too many of the servants had felt the lash of the lady's temper, and all of them hoped that the duke could escape her claws.

Miss Harmon was again the chief topic of conversation tonight in the hall. Most of the men had been forced by the duke into beating the wood in search of the young lady, so the escapade was discussed at great length. A dozen different reasons were suggested for her having become lost, and Spence was forced to bite her lips to prevent herself from telling them what she—mistakenly—thought was the true cause. There was no need to give them a reason for poking fun at the poor young lady. An assignation was viewed with varying degrees of tolerance, Mrs. Johnson condemning roundly, more because she did not wish to see any of her girls thinking to follow the example set by Quality. The fact that Miss Harmon could not see would, however, make her an object of ridicule in their eyes.

Spence slipped quickly upstairs as soon as the servants'

dinner was over, to find that Emily was fast asleep. It was shameful to disturb the rest that she must need after what she had been through, and the abigail was sorely tempted to leave her where she was. She had seen enough of Lady Harmon, however, to realise that it would be the young lady who would be blamed if her ladyship's orders were disobeyed.

Moving about the room quietly, she had everything prepared before rousing Emily, helping her into a modest evening gown of jonquil creped muslin with a sash of deeper yellow, and fastening her strand of small pearls about her throat. The rain had caused the fine hairs about Emily's face to curl, and the abigail made no attempt to confine them, only drawing back the rest of her hair so that it fell down her back. The style made her look even younger than her years, more like a schoolroom miss than a young lady whose first season was behind her.

Maybe her ladyship will remember that she's not much more than a babe, after all, and will send her back to bed, Spence told herself, not believing for an instant that Lady Harmon would be so thoughtful of her daughter.

Lady Harmon would not—not when it seemed that her schemes for Emily were about to bear fruit. When the party below stairs had been gathering for dinner, her ladyship had approached the viscount and had said in honeyed tones, "I cannot thank you enough, Lord Stearnes, for your rescue of my little girl, and I know that her father extends his thanks as well. Emily is resting now, but she will wish to add her own thanks to ours when she comes downstairs later this evening."

Having been warned to expect what he thought would most likely be an attack from the dangerous chit who had been responsible for the ruin of his clothes as well as of Lady Isobel's gown, Arthur took on a hunted look. It seemed to him that the fat old female—and doubtless the young one, as well—had plans for making him a tenant-for-life.

When he realised that Philip would not allow him to get

near Isobel—unable to recognise that it was she who clung to the duke and not the other way about—he had made his escape as soon as the party rose from the table and fled to the village in search of more congenial, and less dangerous, company.

Lady Harmon did not become aware of his defection until the gentlemen rejoined the ladies, and by that time Emily had come downstairs and was surrounded by her eager friends, who had caught her the moment she entered the saloon and had drawn her aside, begging to be told the details of her being lost in the wood. It was too bad of the viscount not to appear, her ladyship thought, especially when she had told him that Emily would be here. She would just have to thank him another time.

Perhaps it would have been better, after all, if she had insisted that Emily come down to dinner, so that Lord Stearnes could have sympathised with her for her experience and could have been impressed at once with the fact that Emily felt that she owed her life to him. Once he had heard that, it would be only natural for him to wish to take that life into his keeping.

"I went for a walk and lost my way," Emily was saying in response to anxious enquiries from her friends. The statement sounded weak even to her, but she preferred not to mention that she had gone to sleep and then had been frightened by the storm.

"But you *said* you were going to your room to rest," Laura objected. "Emily, were you—did you—go out to meet someone?" What a delightful bit of gossip that would make—mild, innocent-appearing Emily involved in an assignation.

Emily was horrified at the question. That her friends would think her capable of such shameless behaviour as that. . . . Of course, there had been the episode with Philip, but that had not been of her making. Still, if Philip had wished for her to meet him, would she not have done so without another thought?

"No, no," she said so emphatically that Laura laughed and the other girls were certain that their suspicions were correct. "I did . . . go to my room . . . but . . . but my migraine was worse than before, and I thought that some air might make it better."

She was not a good liar, and the colour which rose to her face as she said these words was enough to convince all of her friends that there must be a man involved. But who could it be? All the members of the house party had still been on hand when the search was begun.

Could she have met someone—someone of whom her parents would not approve—during the time she had been separated from them at the fair? Was that the reason it had taken the rest of them so long to find her? She had not known that they were intending to stop there, so *that* meeting would have had to have been accidental. Was it someone she had known before or someone new? And of course she had stolen out this afternoon to meet him.

Clever Emily! Her friends looked at her with new respect and forbore to question her further just now, although each of them resolved to gain her confidence and hear the *true* story the moment they were freed from parental supervision.

Unaware of the suspicions she had aroused, Emily was trying to nerve herself for the coming interview with Arthur. Was her mama right? Would he be pleased at being told how heroic she thought his rescue had been? He had appeared to be anything but pleased when he had found her, but that might have been because he had been worried for her safety. Certainly, Mama ought to know the best way for her to act, she thought, forgetting how wrong her mama had always been about anything concerning her sight and her spectacles.

She found herself wishing that, instead of Arthur, it had been the mysterious Philip who had rescued her once again. Would he—would he have kissed her if he had come upon her there in the wood? Her colour flared anew at the thought of his wonderful kisses, and her friends nudged one another, suspecting rightly that she was thinking of a man, but guessing wrongly that it must be the one she had gone to meet today.

Arthur had certainly shown no indication of wishing to kiss her, Emily recalled, even when she had thrown herself at him. Probably, no gentleman would behave in such a fashion when he found a young lady in distress. Which made her all the more certain that Philip must be completely ineligible and that the sooner she banished him from her thoughts, the better it would be.

Since it was most unlikely that she would ever see him again—that is, meet him again, for she had not truly seen him—it would be best for her to concentrate upon what she intended to say to Arthur.

It was not until the party was breaking up to go to bed that she found herself near the garishly dressed figure whom she mistook for that of the viscount. There would be no better opportunity than this, she thought, and approached him shyly.

"I must . . . that is, I *wish* to say how happy I am that you came to search for me today."

Sir John smiled. It was true that he had taken part in the search, for Durban had made it clear that only the older gentlemen would be excused from the task, and the baronet had no wish to be classed among them. He had gone about the search in a halfhearted way, however, as he had as little desire to have his clothing spoilt as the viscount had and had managed to keep only to the well-travelled tracks.

Since he had been so careful to avoid thorny bushes or boggy spots that might ruin the shine of his boots, not even he could have considered his role an important one. The fact that, of all the party, the girl had singled him out for her thanks could mean only one thing. She was ripe for a bit of dalliance, and he would be happy to oblige her. Thanks to the housekeeper's vigilance, things had been dull for a man of his tendencies since he had come to Maidencourt.

In common with Emily's friends, he was certain that her only purpose in slipping off to the wood was to meet a man, but he must have proven an unsatisfactory lover if she was so soon in search of another. Not that he was surprised. Songs about love in the greenwood were all very well, but only a lout would choose so uncomfortable a location for his sport. And a lout he must have been to have left her alone in the storm—or had he only fled when it was clear that she was discovered? Not that it mattered now.

Tucking her hand within the bend of his arm and patting it, he said, "There is nothing that would give me more pleasure than the opportunity of serving you, my dear." He smirked, certain that one so free with her favours would recognise the double entendre.

The warmth in his tone surprised Emily, as did his words, which she had *not* understood, of course. What she had thought was indifference on the viscount's part was nothing more than shyness, it would seem. He had been interested in her after all, but had been afraid to speak without some sign from her. If only she had spoken to him sooner in this manner, everything might have been settled by this time—to Mama's satisfaction, at least.

Emily did not see that he had drawn her aside to allow the others to mount the stairs ahead of them, but Barham was certain that she was agreeable to his scheme. Arm in arm, they went up the stairs as the servants began to put out the lights behind them. It was so comfortable, Emily thought, to have someone guide her, so that she need not fear falling over anything in the hall.

"I have been hoping for a chance to know you better," Sir John said as they walked along the upper hallway. "But I had no idea that you felt the same."

"Oh, I do indeed," Emily assured him. That was not entirely true; not true at all, she thought, recalling Philip, then crushing down that memory. She must forget about him; must encourage Arthur as Mama had ordered her to do.

"If I had known that, my dear, we need not have wasted so much time."

"Yes, but you can understand that I did not wish to be the one to speak out." It was difficult to count the steps along the hall to her own doorway while they were talking, but she was certain that she had made no mistake.

"This is my room," she said, her shyness returning. Somehow, even if this was his parents' home, and even if she was to fix his interest, it did not seem quite proper for any gentlemen to be here, so near to her bedroom. She was aware, because Violet had explained the arrangements, that they were situated along a different hallway than the rooms of the ladies.

"I know." He had considered taking her to his own room, but since the minx had led him here, she must know that they would be undisturbed, so he had no objection if she preferred her own bed.

Her hand was still being tightly held under his arm, and now he had put his own hand over it. Emily tugged hers free, saying, "Thank you once more for seeing me upstairs, but I fear it is growing quite late. Perhaps we can talk more tomorrow, Lord Stearnes."

"Lord Stearnes? Oh, no—you have the name wrong, my dear." That little fool Violet had gabbled the names when introducing them, so it was no wonder if she had made a mistake. Without Emily's being certain exactly how he had managed to do so, he had pushed her into the room and had come in with her. "Names are unimportant at such a time, to be sure, but I should like to hear mine on your tongue. It is John; let me hear you say it."

"John?" Then she had been talking to the wrong gentleman. This was Violet's beau, not the viscount. Too late, she remembered that the two dressed much in the same fashion, as far as she had been able to tell. But if he was Sir John, what was he doing *here*, in her bedroom, of all places? She heard the click of the latch as he closed the door behind

him, and her voice rose almost to a shriek. "You are not
—you cannot come—"

"Oh, but I most certainly can, and you are the one who
must realise that you cannot . . . cannot throw out lures as
you have been doing and then expect to dismiss me with no
more than a handshake. That is not what you had in mind
when you spoke to me, and both of us know it, so it is too
late now for you to pretend to be coy. Come, my dear, we
have the entire night before us, and I am certain that you will
enjoy it as much as I, once you admit that you want me."

Emily opened her mouth to scream but, sensing her intention, he clapped his hand over her lips, saying roughly,
"None of that, now. You wished me to come here and I am
staying." She moaned and struggled as he half-carried, half-
dragged her across the room toward the bed.

Spence, who had been dozing in the corner while waiting
to put the young lady to bed, was aroused by the noise and
sprang up in alarm when she saw the girl was helpless in the
arms of Rake Barham.

"Leave her be, you—you monster!" she cried shrilly,
flinging herself upon the man and attempting to pull his
arms from about his victim.

Startled by the attack, for he had supposed they were alone
in the room, Sir John cried, "Get out of here," and struck
her so that she staggered across the room.

His action gave Emily the opportunity to wrench free from
his grasp, and she began to scream in earnest. Spence added
her outcries to those of the young lady, and in a moment the
room was filled with people in various stages of undress.

"What is going on here?" the earl thundered, having
been prodded into speech by his wife.

When she pulled away from Sir John's embrace, Emily had
fallen against the bedpost and was clinging to it for support.
"He—he forced his way into my room," she gasped.

"Nothing of the sort," the baronet retorted. "She invited
me in, then made a scene when I accepted."

His indignation was genuine, for the girl *had* approached him. His career had been a varied one, but he had never encounted a situation such as this.

"Oh, Emily," Violet wailed. "How could you do this? I thought that you were my friend." Bursting into tears, she flung herself into her mother's arms. Over her head, the countess turned an icy glare, first upon Emily, then upon Sir John.

"I think it would be wisest if you were to leave here the first thing in the morning," she declared. "Both of you. I do not know what the custom may be in other houses, and I do not wish to know, but we do not allow this kind of thing at Maidencourt."

Both the girl and the baronet started to speak, but Lady Montayne went on, addressing Emily. "I need not tell you how disappointed I am in your conduct." She spoke only the truth, for she had come to think that Emily would make an excellent daughter-in-law. Now, to discover that she was the sort to invite a gentleman into her bedroom. . . .

"My lady—" Spence began, coming forward to Emily's defence, but she was silenced by a wave of the countess's hand.

"That will do," Lady Montayne ordered. "You have been lax, Spence, lax indeed, in not reporting to me at once the . . . unladylike . . . behaviour that Miss Harmon must have been displaying. It is clear enough that the . . . that Sir John would not have acted as he did if the girl had not given him some encouragement, and I think—"

"But I did not," Emily sobbed, but was too overset to go on, to explain that she had thought she was speaking to Arthur.

"That will do," her hostess said again. "I must blame myself in part for this . . . matter. I should not have invited you and your parents without having made a thorough investigation first." She forgot conveniently that she *had* checked upon the Harmons and had found them eligible before she had issued the invitation. "Instead, merely because my poor daughter took a liking to you. . . . She was fooled, as I was myself, and I do not have the excuse of being a credulous young girl. It is a mistake that I shall not make again. Come, Violet." She left, almost carrying her still-weeping daughter.

The earl stayed behind long enough to pat Emily's hand and to say, "Never you mind, child. I don't believe a word of it, and I'll see that Miranda changes her tune."

Then he, too, was gone and, since Sir John had taken the opportunity to slip away some time before, the other watchers began to drift away, for it seemed that nothing more would happen. Emily was left alone with her parents and Spence. For a moment, Lady Harmon's anger left her almost speechless—but not entirely so. Glaring at Spence as if she held the woman partly responsible for what had occurred, or at least for the fact that it had been made public knowledge, she ordered, "You will pack my daughter's things at once—at once, do you hear? Come, Harmon, we must see to our own packing."

"But—" his lordship began helplessly, feeling that to go away would be to admit Emily's guilt. He was overborne.

"We shall leave immediately. I refuse to spend a moment longer than is necessary under this roof. That woman— saying that we should have been *investigated*." She waddled angrily out of the room, her husband trailing after her like an unhappy shadow.

Spence went to Emily and put both arms about her, saying, "There, miss, don't be in such a taking. Things will be better soon." If her fat ladyship had any feeling at all, she would be here now, comforting the child instead of flying into the boughs over what the countess had said. And *she* ought to have been more understanding and to have listened to Miss Harmon, the abigail thought disloyally.

"No, no, they will not. They will never be better. Everyone thinks . . . and I did not—"

"Of course you did not. The gentleman was entirely to blame, I'm sure; remember that I saw him. *Gentleman*! We all know what he is, every one of us in the servants' hall. What her ladyship—the countess, I mean—was thinking of to allow Lady Violet to moon over him as she did, I cannot imagine. We're well rid of him, I can tell you. And your mama will soon stop scolding about it."

"No, she will not. Right now, she is angry at the countess for being angry with me. But before long, everything will be my fault. It always is. And this time she is right. She had such plans for me, and now I am ruined. I can never find a husband now."

"You are not ruined, not a bit of it," Spence said, patting her shoulder. "You needn't think the family is going to let a word of this get out—not with the way Lady Violet has been chasing him."

"*They* may not say anything, but you know that Laura and Marjorie will spread the story as quickly as they can. They think such terrible things about me already—that I was meeting a *man* in the wood. And probably Arthur's friends will talk as well; I am certain that they gossip as much as the girls do."

She went into a fresh burst of tears, and Spence, who knew only too well that she was right about the gossipmongers, could only hold her until she had quieted a bit. Then she fetched a damp cloth and made Emily lie upon the bed, the cloth over her eyes, bidding her rest while the packing was being done. She smiled to herself when she saw that, despite her unhappiness, the girl had fallen asleep.

"If her mama had only had the good sense to let her stay up here and sleep when she should have done, none of this would have happened," she said softly to herself, resolved to allow Emily to rest as long as possible. When Lady Harmon called for her daughter to leave, it would be time enough to rouse her.

* * *

Along with everyone else in the house party, the duke had been drawn to the room by Emily's screams. Since she had certainly been in no need of help by the time he arrived—if she had ever been—he had stood silently in the background, listening to the charges being interchanged. Gillian and Morely had stood near him, making remarks—none of them complimentary to Emily, although they had intended them to be.

"She's a downy one, all right," one of them had said. "Going off today to meet someone in the wood—"

"And now this. Wonder why she went to screaming, though. She'd have known what Barham had in mind when she invited him in."

"Didn't know that the servant would be on hand, of course. Set up a howl when she saw her, to make it look as if he had been trying to take advantage of her."

The countess had come out of the room at that moment with her daughter in tow, and the two young men had fallen silent. Stepping aside to allow his aunt to pass, Durban had turned and gone back to his room, determined to put the matter out of his mind.

This, he found, was beyond his powers. Striding back and forth across the room, kicking aside a stool that stood in his way, he cursed softly but fluently. That he, with all his experience with females, should have been so easily taken in by a pair of clinging arms and soft lips.

How eagerly she had come into his embrace. He had been surprised at the time, but too pleased to wonder about it until later, when he had realised that the girl had not recognised him. Now he began to wonder once more. *Would* she have behaved in the same manner, no matter whose arms had been holding her? It was beginning to look as if that was what she would have done.

He had felt sorry for her this afternoon, believing that she had truly been lost in the wood, but now even that episode was suspicious. Was the girl so free as that with her favours? This thing with Barham; anyone could see the sort he was.

Abruptly, he stopped his pacing, pounding his fist upon the bedpost. That was it. Anyone *could* see—anyone except Emily. He remembered her protest—"he forced his way in"—and thought of how quickly Barham had made himself scarce when the trouble began.

Walking down the hallway, the duke tapped at a door and went in without waiting for a reply.

"Barham," he said, "I'd like a word with you."

═13═

EMILY'S FEARS WERE justified. She was in deeper disgrace than she had ever been in a life filled with moments her mama considered disgraceful. The Harmon family had left Maidencourt quietly at dawn, before any of the others of the party were awake.

Only Lady Harmon's fear of highwaymen had prevented their leaving as soon as their cases were packed, and she might well have preferred the danger of being robbed to spending several more hours beneath the roof where all her plans had been shattered and her family had been so cruelly insulted.

"Who are the Leslies, anyhow?" she stormed, forgetting for the moment how anxious she had been for an alliance with the family. "Before one of them—doubtless no better than he should have been—dangled after Queen Elizabeth and was well paid for it? One of *my* ancestors was with the Conqueror, and the Harmons can trace their line almost as far. I shall not stay here another moment to be so insulted by—why, she is not much more than a mushroom."

Ignoring the slur upon his host's ancestry, which was truly illustrious, and forbearing to remind his lady that not *all* of the Conqueror's companions had been noble, Lord Harmon—his foremost thought being for his own comfort —tactfully pointed out that such a hasty departure as her ladyship was planning would be certain to set the servants to gossiping about its cause.

Grudgingly, her ladyship agreed to delay their departure for the few hours until daylight.

The lifelong habit of pretending that the servants must not know that anything was amiss, even when it was obvious that they did know—especially in this case, when Hough was one of the interested spectators at the scene and would certainly give her version of what she had heard to the others, was even more compelling than her indignation.

This same pretence forced her to contain her wrath during the journey to Harmon Hall, while Emily huddled in a corner of the carriage, weeping once more and with her head throbbing from the tears she had shed last night. Lord Harmon sat in uncomfortable silence, thinking of the scenes that were to come.

His foreboding was not without cause. The moment the trio entered the Hall, her ladyship ordered all the servants away. This unprecedented behaviour made them linger out of sight but within earshot, eager to hear any hint of scandal.

Left—theoretically—alone with her family, Lady Harmon began her tirade. She started by directing her libels at the countess, first belittling that lady's pedigree most shamefully, then turning to the earl's family.

She speculated at length upon precisely the sort of service the long-dead Sir Edmund might have rendered to his Queen to have been so well rewarded, then proceeded, generation by generation, to the present day, commenting in scandalous fashion upon the probable reasons for their rise in rank. Even the present duke came in for his share of calumny, although Lady Harmon had no personal reason for condemning his style of life, and he had been kind to Emily. That, however, was not enough to save him from her catalogue of wrongs.

Her wrath had not in the least abated when she had finished with the Leslies, and she turned upon Emily, berating her for her stupidity in getting herself into such a coil.

Trembling, almost unable to speak by this time, Emily whispered, "A mistake—"

"And what were you about, to allow a mistake of that sort to occur? Certainly you know you ought not to have been speaking to the man. And how did he know where your bedroom was, if you did not tell him?"

"He walked—we came upstairs together."

"That is precisely what I mean. How could you—a girl of your upbringing—allow him to accompany you? You are not so green that you would not know that a man of that sort would take such behaviour on your part as an invitation to make advances. . . ." It did not occur to her ladyship that a girl of Emily's upbringing would be exactly that green. Never in her sheltered life had she been permitted to meet a man of Sir John's stamp.

"I did not know—I mean, I thought—" It seemed that Lady Harmon had, for the moment, run out of words or, more likely, out of breath, so Emily said quickly, "I only spoke to him because I thought that he was the viscount."

This was enough to start her ladyship off once more.

"You thought he was the viscount? Emily Harmon, how can you tell such a tale as that and expect anyone to believe you? Lord Stearnes is a *young* man; he and Sir John look nothing alike. Anyone with half an eye can see—"

"That will be quite enough," Lord Harmon said in a tone that no one had heard from him in more than twenty years. His wife stared at him, open-mouthed, surprised into silence by his interruption, and Emily looked in his direction, although she could not see him until he came to her and put an arm about her shoulders.

"The blame is not Emily's," he went on in the same tone, "but yours, Amelia. It was you who would not allow our daughter to wear her spectacles. None of this would have happened—none of the accidents at the house party would have happened—if it had not been that you were so ambitious. You set Emily to dangling after Stearnes when it was clear to anyone—except Emily, who could not see, and you, who refused to do so—that he did not have eyes for anyone except that Darcy woman. I doubt that he even knows Emily is alive.''

Lady Harmon began to bluster, but an impatient gesture from her lord silenced her once more. In the hallway, several of the servants exchanged delighted glances at hearing their domineering mistress receive such a setdown—and from his lordship, who had never been known to raise his voice.

''You tell Emily that she should have known she was not talking to Stearnes. Well, how was she to know that, unless someone told her; and you may be certain that Barham would not have done so, even if he knew she was making a mistake. The way that young fop Stearnes aped Barham's styles, there was no way that she could tell which of them was which with only the colour of their clothes to go by.''

He paused, recalling the time when he had laughed at the doctor for saying much the same thing to him, but he had long since learnt better, even if Amelia had not. Lady Harmon was still too astonished by her husband's strange behaviour to interrupt.

''It was *your* fear that the child would look ridiculous which was to blame, and I was to blame for not overruling you and insisting that Emily be allowed to wear her spectacles. If she had worn them, she would have known that it was Barham who was after her, and she would also have seen young Stearnes for the nodcock he is, which is something you could not see, with your excellent eyesight.''

Overwhelmed by his words, Emily could only gasp, ''Oh, Papa,'' and fling herself upon his chest, threatening to dissolve into tears once more. Fearing this, he patted her shoulder awkwardly, for he was not in the habit of showing his affection, and said, ''There, my pretty, no need for you to cry anymore, and no need of anymore taking on over what happened. It cannot be helped, but never think that you are ruined, no matter what some busybodies may say. As for Stearnes, you are much better off without him. *I* would never have agreed to such a match.''

''Harmon—'' her ladyship began, forgetting her recent distribe against the viscount's family and preparing to argue that it would have been an excellent match, one which any family would be proud to have made.

Lord Harmon, however, had not finished. ''And nothing of the sort will happen again, for you may wear your spectacles whenever you please.''

Over Emily's shoulder, he cast so stern a look at Lady Harmon that she, who had ruled the roost since the day of her marriage and who had never been overruled by her usually compliant husband except once—and that in the matter of purchasing Emily's spectacles—found herself agreeing weakly.

''And nothing more will be said about any of the things that happened while we were at Maidencourt,'' he said, pursuing his advantage and winning another agreement.

In the days that followed, Emily went about the Hall, enjoying the fact that she could wear her spectacles whenever she liked, and putting the unhappiness of the past days quickly out of her mind. It was less easy to forget the few moments of true happiness she had experienced there—the precious moments she had spent in Philip's arms, feeling the thrill of his kisses and the warmth they had sent all through her—but she told herself each time the memory recurred, which was seldom more than once an hour, that she must forget that as well.

She would never see him again. Actually, she had never seen him at all. If only she had worn her spectacles that day so that she might have seen his face, might have the sight of it to treasure as well as the blissful memory of his embrace.

Still, if she *had* worn her spectacles, she doubtless would have been able to keep up with the other riders and would not have fallen from her horse. Even if she had fallen and Philip had come to her rescue, the spectacles would certainly have given him a disgust of her. Better not to have seen his face than not to have known his kisses.

Emily sighed, telling herself she was foolish indeed to continue to think of him. Nothing could come of such dreams. Even if she could never love anyone else, and she knew that she could not, it was a girl's duty to marry.

So when the next season came around, she would probably put away her spectacles and allow her mama to take her to London again in search of an eligible *parti*. That would please Mama, but could *she* bear to marry anyone else when her heart would always belong to Philip?

Lady Harmon had kept her word to say nothing, but she frowned ominously whenever she saw her daughter in her spectacles. They were a constant reminder to her of Emily's failure to attach the viscount. Emily was aware of her mama's disapproval, but she ignored it—Mama was in the habit of disapproving of almost everything her daughter did, anyhow—as long as she had Papa's permission to wear them. If only she had been allowed to wear them while they were visiting at Maidencourt, she would not have spilt the tea on Lady Isobel, or stabbed Sir Hayden with her needle, or spoken to Sir John.

On the other hand—how her mind forever came back to that—she might not have tumbled from her horse and been rescued by Philip. Resolutely, she pushed the thought away for at least the dozenth time in the past few days, and forced herself to think instead of how wonderful it was to be able to see everything about her. Even that, however, lacked the thrill it had held before. . . .

The habit of obedience to her mama's orders was so strong that, despite her papa's permission, the sound of carriage wheels upon the drive made her snatch off her spectacles. She hid them beneath the piece of needlework from which she had been ripping out the stitches that had been put in the wrong place at Maidencourt before she turned unseeing eyes in the direction of the newcomer.

Drawing his pair of matched blacks to a halt before the door of the Hall, the Duke of Durban glanced down at the scraped knuckles of the hand that held the ribbons and smiled somewhat grimly. He had been forced to darken both of Barham's eyes, and had enjoyed the task, before the man would admit that the Harmon girl had not actually invited him into her room. Even then, however, Sir John had stoutly maintained that *anyone* might have behaved as he had done in the circumstances.

"If you ask me," he declared, "the chit's attic is to let. She seemed to think I was Stearnes."

He was of the opinion that his admission to the duke was sufficient, for surely Durban was man of the world enough to appreciate the situation; it had taken additional physical persuasion to make him repeat the story for the assembled family and guests, all of whom Durban had ruthlessly routed from their beds. When some of them, Isobel in particular, had maintained that Emily could scarcely have mistaken the two men (Arthur preened himself on the fact that she no longer considered him a boy), Durban told them what he suspected about Emily's near-sightedness. He was careful, however, not to hint at the occasion that had given him the first inkling of her condition. When called upon, Spence was more than willing to corroborate his story of the girl's affected vision.

Almost everyone agreed that an apology was due to Miss Harmon for their unjust suspicions of her, but it was learnt that she and her family had left Maidencourt during the time it had taken the duke to persuade Barham to speak. Violet burst into tears at hearing this, declaring that she would never forgive herself for having treated her dear friend so badly. She had to be consoled once more by the countess, who was happy at the thought that her first opinion of the young lady's character was the correct one after all.

Laura and Marjorie nudged one another, thinking enviously that Emily had been the intended victim of a ravisher, rescued just in time. Exactly as these things occurred in the best Minerva romances—except that there had been no hero to rescue her, only a servant and the members of the house party.

Only two members of the entire party did not feel in sympathy with the departed Emily. Lord Stearnes still blamed her for the ruin of his finery and now had a new grievance. The chit was the cause—however innocent she might have been—of bringing into disfavour a man he had long admired and attempted to copy.

Lady Isobel was beginning to suspect that there might be a deeper reason for the duke's continued chivalry toward the troublesome girl. He had defended her from the first—and now had actually stooped to fighting over her, like some common street brawler instead of a peer of the realm. She would have a great deal to say to him on *that* subject when they were alone.

Sir John would doubtless have agreed with them in disliking Emily, but he had wisely made his escape at the first moment Durban's eye was off him. Throwing his fashionable wardrobe together with a lack of consideration for its condition, which would have appalled him at any other time, he paused only long enough to snatch up several small figurines. He might be able to pawn them to stave off his worst creditors.

The chit—taking up with me because she thought I was *Stearnes*, he told himself bitterly. This would be a lesson to him to steer clear of the infantry in the future. Middleham's widow was fairly well inlaid. A cit's widow, to be sure, but a rich one. . . . There came a time when a man could no longer afford to be particular.

All of this, including the duke's unpleasant but final interview with Isobel, had happened two days ago, and now, as

172

he dismounted from his curricle and handed the ribbons to the groom who had hurried to take them, the duke was wondering why he had come. Either he or the earl could have franked Violet's letter, but he had offered to carry it for her. During the entire journey, he had been telling himself that he was coming only because he was the head of the family and it was therefore his duty to apologise to the Harmons for the treatment they had received at Maidencourt.

Spying the slim figure upon the terrace, he waved away the butler's determined attempt to guide him into the house, merely tossing his curly-brimmed hat to the man before striding off to face Emily.

"Miss Harmon," he began, then caught himself, amazed at the words which threatened to tumble from his lips. Darling, precious, sweetheart—he wanted to call her all these, and so much more. Of course. *That* was why he had come; he ought to have realised that from the first moment he had held her in his arms, instead of having his doubts about her. He should have been certain, when she was lost in the wood, that his concern had not been for *a* girl, but for *his* girl.

Still, he must not shock her by saying anything of the sort —so soon. There was time enough to woo her properly. "I have a letter for you," he said awkwardly.

"Oh, thank you." Emily frowned slightly, puzzled by the voice. She was certain that she had heard it before, but was unable to identify the speaker. A courier, perhaps, or a servant, although not one of the Hall staff.

Durban proffered the letter, but she stood with her hand outstretched, making no move to take it from him. His suspicions about her eyesight confirmed, the duke put the missive into her hand, and a tender smile curved his lips as he watched her bring it close to her eyes. His vain little darling, he thought, still trying to hide her problem from the world. He pitied her now; his cousin's scrawl—certainly no tribute to the efforts of several expensive governesses—was difficult enough to read at the best of times.

Dear Emily, Violet had written, *I thought that I should never be able to forgive you after having seen John in your room, but now I do so freely. He has admitted that you were not to blame for what happened, so I am sorry that I suspected you—but he was always so charming I thought you must see him as I did.*

Emily shook her head. Even now, Violet did not remember that she could not have seen Sir John.

It was the best thing that could have happened after all, for it has made me see that he is not at all what I thought him to be. He has left, and I hope never to see him again.

This did not sound like the letter of a heartbroken girl. Emily wondered if she had read it aright, and went back over what she had read, only to find there was no change.

Mama and Papa have agreed to take me to Brighton, which should be very gay, as the Prince is there. Not that I should be allowed to join his set, nor would I wish to. But I am greatly surprised, for James—I should say Mr. Gillian —has said he will be there, although I am certain that he never said anything before this about going. I did not realise before what a handsome young man he really is, and he has been so kind to me. I must tell you that Mama fairly dotes on him, despite his being a younger son, and he has given Papa some good advice upon his roses. Do not be surprised, dear Emily, if I have some exciting news soon. I am so happy, and I hope we can be friends again.

The most amazing thing has happened—scandalous, really. Papa is so vexed with Arthur and threatens to cut him off, which, of course, he cannot do. Arthur has eloped—and with Lady Isobel Darcy, of all people—

Emily glanced up from the letter, supposing that the messenger was still present, for she had not heard him leave.

"I am so happy for Violet," she said, forgetting that she ought not to be confiding in this man, who, after all, might only be a servant. But she felt that she must speak to someone, and he was the nearest. "She could not have cared too much for Sir John, or she could not have found a new interest in only a few days. And now that she knows Sir John's true nature. . . . But I am happy that she knows that I did not try to attract him."

"No, you were trying to attract the viscount." Why must he remind himself of that? Durban wondered. The thought that she had done so rankled, even when he reminded himself that she could not have seen what a fool Arthur really was. But would she be unhappy at his elopement?

She was thinking that this man had no right to have any opinion about what she had done, but she imagined that she had heard censure in his voice. Well-accustomed to being blamed for things, even though they were not of her making, she said quickly, "Only because Mama said that I should do so."

Durban felt as if a great weight had been lifted from his mind by the words.

"I truly did not know him. He scarcely spoke to me all the time I was there. Papa has said that we should not have suited, and I think he is right. He said, too, that Arth—the viscount—was always interested in Lady Isobel, but I did not think that she cared for him."

So Violet had told her that as well. Good; he would be saved from having to say that Isobel was no longer in their way. "It is rather that, having lost her opportunity of becoming a duchess," said Durban, "Isobel decided that being a countess one day was the best thing she could do at this late date and seized Arthur before the young bubble-head could become disenchanted with her, too."

"What do you mean?" This man seemed to be talking in some sort of riddles.

Only a short time ago, when he had first realised his true feelings for the girl, the duke had resolved to court her slowly, to win her interest bit by bit, to convince her that he, and not Arthur, was the man for her. Now, seeing her up-turned face so near to his, pansy-coloured eyes trying to see his expression, her lips so inviting, his good intentions vanished and he stepped closer to take her in his arms.

"No!" Emily cried, trying for an instant to struggle against his embrace, thinking in panic that Sir John had somehow sought her out. Then, as his lips covered her own, she knew who he must be and clung to him, returning his kisses eagerly, even while she felt that they were drawing her out of herself, so that she was no longer a person, but only a part of him. This time, she knew she would never let him go, no matter what her parents might say of him.

"Oh," she gasped when she was able to speak once more, "you are the one who kissed me before."

"Certainly. I hope," he said with a sternness that was only partly assumed, although her kiss had almost routed the last of his doubts, "that you are not in the habit of allowing just *anyone* to kiss you."

"Of course I am not," she said indignantly. "Only you."

"Then—" He started to draw her close once more, but she freed herself from his arms, saying, "Just wait for a moment."

Fumbling for the table, she found her hidden spectacles and set them upon her nose. If they gave him a disgust of her as her mama had foretold, she knew she would die. But he must know the truth about her. Facing him once more, she broke into a laugh of pure delight.

"Why, you are beautiful," she said wonderingly, letting her gaze roam over his fair hair, the eyes which—even now—held so tender a look for her, his lips which gave her such wondrous pleasure.

Philip laughed a bit self-consciously. "Gentlemen are not beautiful."

"You are . . . you are . . . the most beautiful man I have ever seen." Of course, she had *seen* so few, but no one, seen or not, could compare with him. She put a hand to her spectacles. "You do not mind . . . about . . . about these?"

"Mind? Certainly not. It was quite clear during the house

party when you wandered into one mull after the other that you could not see, and I thought it shameful that your parents would not have you fitted for spectacles. I even considered offering to do so myself. Your eyes, my darling, are the loveliest I have ever seen, but they do get you into all kinds of trouble.''

"I know." She was not surprised he knew everything that had happened. "Like spilling the tea—''

"And speaking to the wrong man.''

"Yes, that was frightening. But of course, any of *them* would have been the wrong man. Papa bought these spectacles for me some months ago when a doctor convinced him that I should have them. But Mama has forbidden me to wear them in public. She says that no gentleman would offer—'' She broke off, clapping her hands to her mouth, colouring in her confusion.

Philip's laugh was tender as he drew her into his arms once more. "There are a great many things that I am certain your mama does not know; among them, my angel, is how very much I love you. And that I do intend to offer for you—just as soon as I have an opportunity to speak to your father.''

"You do?'' She hoped that Papa would agree; surely he would do so, if she had a chance to tell him that Philip was the only one she would ever love. Her face was so near to his that there was no need for him to answer in words. Their blissful moment was interrupted by the sound of footsteps approaching across the room behind them, and they moved apart, Emily putting up a hand to straighten the spectacles that had been knocked awry by his caress.

Affronted by the fact that Miss Emily was entertaining a strange gentleman alone, the butler had hurried in search of Lord and Lady Harmon and had apprised them of the fact. Since the gentleman had not seen fit to give his name before approaching their daughter, they made haste to see who it was.

As they came out onto the terrace, her ladyship's eyes immediately went to her daughter's spectacles and, from habit, she said sharply, "Emily, how many times have I told you that you must never wear—" She broke off, feeling her husband's gaze upon her.

"Your pardon, Lady Harmon, if I disagree with you," Philip said, taking Emily's hand in his, "but I must insist that my wife shall wear her spectacles at all times."

"Your wife?" Lady Harmon squeaked.

"Not yet, of course, but very soon. That is, if I have your permission, sir."

Lady Harmon fastened a fearful look upon her husband, recalling his poor opinion of the viscount. What if he should feel the same way about the duke? She felt she would expire if he did so, but his lordship said affably, "Certainly, my boy. Certainly, if that is what Emily wishes."

"Oh, it is, Papa," Emily said happily, moving to place a kiss upon Lord Harmon's cheek, then returning once more to Philip's side and to the circle of his arm. Since Papa did *not* object, her happiness was complete.

All of the things that Lady Harmon, in her anger, had said about the Leslies were forgot now that Emily was to make such an excellent match. Even in her most ambitious dreams, her ladyship had never envisioned her daughter as a *duchess*.

"Your Grace—" she began, but was interrupted by Emily.

"You—you are the duke?"

"Emily, must you behave so foolishly?" Her mama's voice was sharp. When they were alone, she would have a great deal to say to Emily upon the subject of interrupting her elders, but for the moment the most important thing was to convince Durban that his bride-to-be was not the moonling she seemed just now. "You know very well that you were presented to the duke at the house party and met him there more than once."

"Yes, I know—but I never saw him before."

Lady Harmon frowned, but before she could scold her

daughter further for uttering such a piece of nonsense, Philip laughed and said, "And that is why I insist that she wear her spectacles. I want to make certain that my duchess always knows who is making love to her."

Her ladyship gasped at the impropriety of this remark, then gasped a second time as Emily said, "Oh, I am certain I shall always know *that*," and raised her face to his to be convinced again.

It was Lord Harmon who cast a benevolent glance at the unseeing pair and took his wife's arm, saying, "Come, my dear. I think we are not needed here."